A Smoking, Deadly Summer in Indy

E. MARVIN NEVILLE

Order this book online at www.trafford.com
or email orders@trafford.com

Most Trafford titles are also available at major online book retailers.

Printed in the United States of America.

ISBN: 978-1-4269-4842-8 (sc)
ISBN: 978-1-4269-4843-5 (hc)
ISBN: 978-1-4269-4844-2 (e)

Library of Congress Control Number: 2010916840

Trafford rev. 12/08/2010

 www.trafford.com

North America & International
toll-free: 1 888 232 4444 (USA & Canada)
phone: 250 383 6864 ♦ fax: 812 355 4082

To my sweet, luscious Ally Katt:
Without you, this collection would not
have seen the light of day. But, most importantly,
my life would have been snuffed
into darkness.

TABLE OF CONTENTS

THE KISSING LESSON

A Short Story

By

E. Marvin Neville

George Cornwell was sitting in a bar ordering what was quite probably the last scotch on the rocks he'd be able to pay for forever. He loved scotch. He simply drank whatever he could, mostly cheap wine or near bathtub liquor.

George had had two thousand dollars. Life Malone had paid him for one of the easiest favors he'd ever done, so his mouth dropped when he saw the photo of the murdered girl, and her parents, who'd been murdered separately only a few days apart. He'd seen that exact photo of the girl before.

Life Malone was a rags-to-riches story. Born in 1972, Life was the product of a heroin addicted mother, and any one of over two-hundred possible fathers. The only reason that he wasn't born heroin addicted was because his mother's pregnancy was so high risk, that she was hospitalized for the entire seven months. Life was born small, but he came out fighting like dingoes over a joey, and had kept fighting for thirty-five years.

Life started selling weed in middle school. He was probably one of the richest poor boys in high school. His mother had done as well as she could under her drug-fueled circumstances, but there was no way he was bringing a child into the world. Ever.

Well before his high school graduation, Life realized that selling pot wasn't going to get him out of his mother's house. Life switched over to crack dealing as seamlessly as a day trader bought and sold stocks. Life had also been enamored with guerilla warfare, and spy tactics. He'd read as much on the subjects as basement nerds spent time plying obscure fantasy video games. He didn't know why he was so focused on those Tom Clancy book-like issues. He attributed the focus to his ingrown theory that it must have come from his father – whoever he was.

Before his 30th birthday, Life Malone had finally been able to financially extricate himself from the drug game. He sold out, and started a barber shop/beauty salon. He parlayed that effort into four of them. He parlayed the four into shop/salons/cosmetology schools. He moved money from those enterprises into a fresh restaurant – the first actual retail business venture on the downtown canal – called "Life on the Canal". It had all been part of the plan to need nobody. The success of the restaurant proffered him enough cash to start his vision – a topless barber shop/beauty salon with an attached strip joint. With both male and female clientele, the cash rolled in like high tide in Indonesia. Life was a hands-on owner. He had a schedule for visiting all of his businesses, and he followed it like an actuary followed statistics. It was on one of those visits that his life changed forever.

Meena Mehta was an absolutely gorgeous twenty-five year old Indian Muslim whose beauty could fell trees, and topple skyscrapers, but who had no idea of just how much power her beauty afforded her. Like her older sister and younger brother, she was first generation Indian-American, and a twenty generation Muslim. She wouldn't say that she liked being an American more than being an Indian-Muslim, but, in her mind of minds, she couldn't deny the fact that she had more to contribute to the world than spitting out babies (preferably male), and serving her husband (not of her own choosing).

The Mehta family owned one-hundred acres of farmland in Greenfield Indiana. They'd built a compound on the property that housed a family of twenty-six people, grew corn, held pigs and cows, and was truly a business venture meant to propagate their culture. The farm was fairly prosperous, but there was also a siginificant amount of outside income. That was the edict. All adults either worked the farm, or worked outside of the farm, and their income went directly to Meena's father. Schooling was allowed, even for the females, but the income that came from its results went directly to Meena's father. He and his brother drove Mercedes Benzes that were changed every three years. She drove a ten-year old Chevy Barreta that was just road worthy enough to get her back and forth to cosmetology school. A job as a cosmetologist would render at least a small beam of sunshine into her Muslim existence that she saw as oppressive at the least and downright crushing at the most. She wanted to fall in love like in the American books and movies, raise children who had a chance to flourish freely and maybe even host the occasional non- Muslim dinner party. But Meena wasn't stupid. Her parents were narrowing down the list of potential husbands for her as she took every breath, and had been doing so for many years. Prospects in the Americas were like a strand of singularitized solid matter traveling through a Black Hole. They moved fast, were unstable, and were mostly only theory.

Wednesday at the eastside salon/school, Meena had a particularly good day. She smashed every hair, nail, and makeup issue she's confronted with, and her classmates and instructors virtually cheered her on as she sprinted for the finish line for the gold in the

1500 meter race. It was as if Meena Mehta and cosmetology had melded together in the cosmos.

Not even the fact that Meena's car wouldn't start after class extinguished Meena's professional high. She was about to call her father when Life emerged from the salon. He'd always been so striking to her. He was confident, successful, and purely in control.

Life had spent an extra hour at the dojo that day, and an extra fifteen minutes at the shooting range that evening. He, too, had been on that day. Things just seemed to be going well that day without any true effort from him. So when he saw the excruciatingly beautiful Indian girl in the parking lot of the eastside salon, he felt extraordinarily beneficent. She was inside of her car, but her honey brown eyes visually burned through the shield of darkness and glass like the taste of prime rib completely crushes the taste of cricket. It was as if they were glowing out directly to him.

Life's SUV was parked a few dozen yards from Meena's car. He shrugged his shoulders. She'd wanted to roll down her window, but her car had lost too much power to do so. She cracked open her door. "I'm about to call my father," she yelled.

"What's wrong with your car?" he returned.

"I'm not a mechanic. I just know that it won't start. I think I left my parking lights on."

"Well, I could tell that you weren't a mechanic the first time I saw your fingernails. I'm not a mechanic, but I do know how to jump a car battery. Would you like for me to try?"

"Yes, please."

Life brought his truck to her car. By the time he got there, she had the hood up, and a set of anemic-looking jumper cables attached to her battery and ready to go. He cared about her car, but he cared more about his. He removed a set of jumper cables that could've jump started a stealth bomber from the rear of his SUV. After connection, her car engine exploded to life. The smile on her face made his testicles tingle. Her teeth were so moonlit white. There was an awkward silence. "Listen, there's a bar right around the corner. Would you like a drink?" Life asked, almost scared.

"You know I'm Muslim," Meena answered.

"In all honesty, you guys have several religions in one, Miss Mehta."

She was impressed that he knew her name.

"I can only stay for a few minutes."

Life Malone had a Dewer's White Label on the rocks, while Meena Mehta had simple water from the tap. They both felt exponentially comfortable with one another because everything in each of their lives poured out of their mouths like Hydrochloric Acid through silk. Meena picked up Life's half-finished second scotch, and threw it down her throat as if she were putting out a fire. It was her first taste of alcohol ever. It burned both her esophagus, and her soul. "May I order one of those?" she asked. He ordered one for each of them. She emptied the cocktail glass, and coughed almost violently afterward.

"Are you okay?" Life asked, standing. She put up her hand as she half coughed and half laughed. She took a drink of water. When she raised her face her grin was broad and tears were streaming from her eyes.

"I don't know much about the Quran, but doesn't this mean you're going to burn in hell?" he asked.

Meena nodded. "Well, I'll see my father and uncles there," she smiled. The look on her face said I'm not drunk, but I'm definitely a bit tipsy.

"What?"

"My cousin makes this homemade brew from the old country. They know that we women know, but we all act like it's not happening."

"That's weird."

"Not really. Remember, it's we women who carry the honor."

"Yeah, but you carry it on your shoulders for the men."

"See. You know more about the Quran than you thought."

They both laughed so loud that the entire population of the bar took notice of them. Meena got up mildly unsteadily. "It's time for me to go," she giggled.

"Maybe I should take you home," Life offered.

"How are you going to get back?"

"Let me worry about that."

"Thank you for that, but I'm more worried about my elders smelling the liquor on my breath."

"I have a remedy for that. It won't beat a breathalyzer, but it'll definitely beat a smell test as long as the tester's nose isn't in your mouth."

As Meena consumed the breath cover cocktail, Life called for a taxi. "You really don't have to do this," she said

"I know," he answered.

Life gave the taxi driver three-hundred dollars to follow them as he drove her home to Greenfield, and to bring him back to his vehicle. Meena fell asleep, but awoke about halfway to her home.

"You okay?" Life asked

"How do you drink that stuff?" Meena groaned.

"Well, most people don't drink the whole glass in one gulp."

"If you ever see me do that again, please kill me, because that's what my head is doing to me now."

Life smiled. "Does that mean you'll have a drink with me another time?"

"I can't believe I'm saying this, but how about tomorrow?"

"Tomorrow's good but why can't you believe you're saying it?"

Meena sighed. "You know, Life, I've never even kissed a guy."

"Well, I would've reversed the kissing, date thing"

"You're right, but I'm drunk. Anyway, once, when I was thirteen, a Buddhist boy asked me to kiss him, and I said yes. But it doesn't really count as a kiss, because he opened his mouth, and I kept mine closed and he just kind of slobbered over my mouth and chin."

Life laughed.

"Don't laugh." She hit him playfully on his arm. "I was mortified."

"Mortified?"

"Are you making fun of me?"

"Well, considering you're not Ming the Merciless, yes."

They both laughed.

"Did you ever kiss that guy again?" Life asked.

"Oh, no," Meena responded emphatically.

"Embarrassed?"

"No, no. His breath smelled like goat poop."

They both laugh heartily. After more laughing, Meena looked at Life endearingly "Have you ever dated women outside of your race?" she asked.

"What makes you think I date Black women?" Life smiled

"Well, I assumed."

"No, you're right. And I am a non-discriminatory dater. Mostly White women, but I did once date a Latina lawyer. She was third generation American, though."

"No Asian girls?"

"No. Asian women stepping out of their race is like DNA. There's a one in seven-hundred billion chance that they'll step out with any race other than White people."

"Yeah, they think of White people as gods on earth," Meena moans. And then she suddenly perked up. "Turn right on this road," she said.

Life pulled up about three-hundred yards from her home. Meena would drive the remaining distance. "You're a prince Mr. Life Malone," she smiled. She was so incredibly sexy. For the first time in his life, he felt like he might want to have children.

"I'll be in the city about noon tomorrow, when and where would you like to have that drink?"

"Why don't you come down to my restaurant about at six."

"I'll meet you there," she smiled, and then leaned over and kissed him gently on the lips, slid over as he exited the car, smiled again, waved, and took off. Life watched her until she pulled into the compound. All he could think was: "wow".

Meena had abdicated ownership of Life's mind from the moment she'd delivered the peck on his lips. Through an excruciatingly lengthy wait where each time he glanced at his watch it seemed that it was running backwards. She finally showed up at the restaurant at five forty-five that afternoon. "Would you like a drink, Miss Mehta?" he asked

She grinned. "Please, call me Meena," she said.

"Okay, Meena. Would you like something to drink?"

"Yes. But make sure that it doesn't have any alcohol in it because I'm still reeling from the drink and a half I had last night."

"Fair enough, are you hungry?"

"I haven't eaten in four hours. It's hard to kill six hours when you have nothing to do except wait for that time to end."

They laughed. Life had reserved the best table for them – next to the front window with a view of the canal – and ordered the best dishes in the house. He couldn't believe that she'd never eaten lobster before. They talked until the restaurant closed.

Life walked her to her car. At her car door, she looked up at him, and smiled. Her brown eyes shined as if they were gold, and her teeth were whiter than bleached cotton.

"I'm ready for a kissing lesson, Life Malone," she said.

"A kissing lesson?" he returned, perplexed.

"Yes. Now, I've done a bit of studying by sneaking looks at television. I've noticed that, most of the time, the male actor kisses the female's top lip while she does the same to his bottom lip, and they kind of work their jaws to make it look real. Am I right?"

"You couldn't be more right."

"So I figure that a man with lips as beautiful as yours can show me how it's really done."

Life was floored, but he hoped that she bought his act of keeping his composure. "Okay, so you want to kiss me instructively?" he asked.

"Yes, but I really, really like the instructor."

He was ready to take a bullet for her.

"Okay, you deep kiss where both mouths open and…"

"She slammed her mouth onto his, mouths wide open, tongues thrashing. Life thought that if this was her first kiss, she was absolutely, positively a natural. She'd been born to collect men's souls with the sweetness of her kiss. He melted inside of her mouth.

Over the next six weeks they saw each other every Wednesday, and any other day that she could sneak away. He fell for her hard, and she loved him more than her own mother. They shared everything about their lives, and, after hearing about his past, instead of running for the exit, she fell deeper in love with him. But they never made love. She was scared. But he was good with that. He enjoyed waiting for her. He was like a teenager, except smarter. Meena was more than a keeper. She deserved to be worshipped. And then the worst thing that even Stephen King could've thought of happened.

Class let out early the Wednesday after Memorial Day. He and Meena were making out in his SUV in the parking lot. Her kisses were like licking honey off of a steak to him. Suddenly, she broke away from him, gazing into his eyes as if she wanted to eat him alive. "Do you live far from here?" she asked, panting.

"I live downtown about twenty minutes away," he answered.

"Would you mind if I came by your place for awhile?"

"I would mind that even less than I mind making money."

They rushed to his home with nearly as much fervor as an EMT in an ambulance trying to save a celebrity. Life lived on the canal only a few hundred yards from his restaurant. He loved downtown living, and he was ready to go to the next level of downtown loving. He wanted to be romantic, and give her a tour of his tri-level home, but Meena saw nothing after the front door. She did everything she could to make sure that her open mouth stayed connected to his open mouth.

They stripped naked in his bedroom, and he removed a condom from his night stand with the ease of licking a stray ice cream dollop from his lip, and put it on in a single motion. She stopped, suddenly. "I'm sure you know this, but I'm a virgin. So if I'm not very good, please forgive me." Meena said.

Life plunged inside of her. She was warm, and tight, and she moaned at his every stroke. He wanted to be technically good for her, but all he could do was pump, and prey that his effort to not come too soon would be enough for her to experience maximum enjoyment. He'd rarely had trouble lasting long enough for a woman, and almost never as an adult. For the first time in an eternity, he found himself struggling to keep from coming immediately. Meena felt sexually celestial. It felt as if he was being masturbated by the golden fist of God. He was ready to ask her to marry him. He used two more condoms that night, each experience was better than the one before. He wondered if he could order an engagement ring, and have it delivered before she left.

Life all but begged Meena to stay – at four in the morning as she dressed to leave – but he knew that she couldn't. And as she drove frantically home, all that she could think about was turning back to be with him.

Once home, she attempted to tip quietly up the stairs to her room, when her parents appeared from the hallway. She was startled like a cockroach when the lights are turned on. She spun around, and her father slapped her hard to the floor before she could even get a good look at him. She saw his long, pointed beard sway in the wake of his effort. Meena tried to get up. He struck her again, and then tossed a stack of photographs onto the floor by her face. They were pictures of her and Life over at least three weeks of time. Most of them were of her and him kissing. She looked up at her parents. She fingered through them. The last was of her kissing Life as she'd entered his house only a few hours ago. But Meena felt not an iota of shame. Instead, she felt horrific anger. "You had me followed?" she asked through the blood streaming from her bottom lip.

"You shamed our family!" her father screamed.

Meena was ready to scream back at him, but then she became oddly calm. She picked up the picture of her and Life entering his home, and stood up. "No, I shamed myself by not telling you how I've felt all these years," she said.

"What do you mean?" her mother asked through tears that spoke volumes.

Meena explained to them how she'd never liked the life they'd provided for her. She was grateful, but it never seemed fair that the women couldn't shoot for their dreams. She wanted to shoot for hers and being with Life Malone was a huge part of that shot. Her father looked down, and then back up at her as softly as a dictator could. "Your aunt is sick. You and your mother are going to India tomorrow. You'll help your mother take care of her sister," he said.

Meena wanted to protest hard, but she did love her aunt. "How long will we be there?" she asked.

"It'll be a few days. We'll talk about this when you get back."

Meena was looking forward to the talk. She had much to say. She called Life.

Life was worried. It had been two weeks and he hadn't heard a peep from Meena. He was thirty-five years old and in love for the very first time. He knew that her family circumstance was tough, but he couldn't help but to feel that she'd been able to knife through it before. Why not now? He'd been checking his cell phone caller ID nearly every minute after he'd awakened from the best sleep he could recall after making love to Meena. He was in the office of his restaurant when a bus boy came back and told him that there was an Indian woman looking for him in the front. He was almost orgasmic with happiness. He rushed to the front of the restaurant as coolly as he could. When he saw her, he was ready to dive onto her. But then he noticed something. The woman waiting for him looked a great deal like Meena, but it wasn't her.

"May I help you?" he asked

"No. I think that I can help you," she answered. "I'm Meena's sister, Jassi."

"She's mentioned you."

"Yes. And she'd mentioned you hundreds of times."

"She'd?"

"Mr. Malone, Meena's dead," Jassi said as she did her best to hold back her emotions. She failed miserably.

"What?" Life asked as he almost fainted and vomited simultaneously.

"Perhaps we should go somewhere more private."

Life and Jassi stepped out onto the canal. It was a fabulously gorgeous Central Indiana night, and Life felt it was being wasted on bad news. He had no idea.

Jassi wasted no time. "My parents had Meena killed," she said.

"What? Why?"

"I think you know why."

"Okay, but I didn't mean for this to happen."

"Of course you didn't. Meena wanted out of this life. Many of us do. You helped her to the best level."

"Helped her? She'd dead."

"And how do you range it, Mr. Malone? Should she have married a fifty-year old man that she'd never met, fought to be with a man who represented the life she really wanted to live, or died?"

"I'm not that smart."

"I'm here because I know how Meena was, and how much she loved you. And that your own life might be in danger."

"Excuse me?"

"If you were in India, you'd be dead by now, Mr. Malone," Jassi almost cried.

"You don't know much about me, do you?" Life asked."

"I know only what Meena told me in secret," she returned. "That's pretty much the way it is in our world, Mr. Malone. "I'm sorry."

15

"Why are you sorry? Do you want me to die?"

"If they were watching you right now, I wouldn't be here. Meena loved you so much. I just thought it was fair to let you know all that I know," Jassi said as she turned and walked quickly away.

Life had seen the compound a number of times after following Meena home. But his guerilla war tactics were heavily required to know where to go once inside. Finding the blueprint of the layout was easy. Finding who would be sleeping where was more difficult. He spent an entire day studying Muslim culture just to be as certain as possible.

Other words Meena had said to him the night they'd made love resonated through his mind like the swinging of the giant pendulum at the Indiana State Museum. "Please don't be gentle with me." He'd cut a swath through the fence in a matter of seconds.

Life crept around the rear of the house. The crickets seemed to be chirping Meena's name. The king of his own Muslim world had locks on the basement windows that could be opened with one swipe of a Slim Jim, protected by an alarm system that could be disengaged with the wave of a flower petal. In less than two minutes, he was in the house.

Life already knew how many people lived in the house, so he knew that the basement was most likely empty. He moved like a snake anyway. His night vision goggles helped tremendously.

He sprayed WD 40 onto the hinges of the basement door, which lead into the kitchen. It slid open like a fried egg in grease. There were seven bedrooms in the house. Three were upstairs, and four were downstairs. The smaller, downstairs bedrooms were packed with very young adults, teenagers, and children. Meena shared a room with a cousin and a niece. Her father and mother, his brother and his wife, and her sister and her husband shared the upstairs. It was an easy call.

Life slipped on his ski mask at the top of the stairs. As he made his way to the far bedroom, he sprayed the hinges of all three doors with WD 40. He slowly opened the door to the far bedroom. He opened the door slightly, but enough to slip halfway into the room. Meena's aunt and uncle were sound asleep, her uncle on his back. Life shot him in the forehead. His wife didn't even stir.

Life crept into the bedroom of Meena's parents. He removed a syringe filled with GHB from his pocket, and injected Meena's mother with most of it. He gave her father just enough to knock him out for a short time, but to leave him paralyzed for at least an hour.

After about fifteen minutes, Meena's father awoke, but was unable to speak or move. He was bound with duct tape. When the haze cleared from his brain, he was horrified to see an entirely black clad man violently sodomizing his wife. When he saw the thick, rich blood on the man's penis, he wanted to scream. But he couldn't. When the man was done, he walked over to him, put the pistol to his head, and then pulled the mask up to expose his face

"I just want you to see the man who can do whatever he wants to you, and your family. But it's not like you'll be able to do anything about it," Life said, matter-of-factly. He put his nose up against Mr. Mehta's. "I'll bet the terror I'm seeing in your eyes right now is nowhere near the terror in your daughter's eyes when you sent five strangers to rape and kill her like the whore you claimed she was." It took three deep breaths for Life to calm himself down, and not unleash on the man in a vicious beating. "You know, Mr. Mehta, I'm not a religious man. I'm a spiritual man. I acknowledge every human beings right to worship as they wish, believe as they wish, do as they wish, and do to themselves whatever they wish as long as it doesn't hurt others. And that's where you and I part company. Only God has the right to take a life from this earth. I don't give a fuck what you THINK Muhammad says only He has that right. And I'd be willing to fight even His right to remove such a beautiful soul such as your daughter from this world. I'd known her for only a very short time, but nobody in my life had ever come close to moving me the way she had." Tears were cascaded down Life's face. He'd experienced much pain in his life, but not having Meena was as if his heart had been blown from his spirit.

Life brandished a knife in his left hand. "I don't believe in Hell, Mr. Mehta. But if I'm wrong, if I wasn't going already, I'll be going after the next sixty-seconds." Life cut a long, deep swath across Mr. Mehta's throat. The blood flowed like the menstrual cycle of the fictional fifty-foot woman, but he didn't die immediately. His eyes exploded with terror and fear as he drowned on his own blood. Life put the gun to his forehead. "I'm going to show you mercy," he said, and he put two bullets into Mr. Mehta's brain.

Life moved very quickly out of the room, and to the third door. He hoped that there was nobody waiting for him there, but he was ready if they were. He put his ski mask, and night goggles back on, and slipped half of his upper body into the room. They weren't. Meena's sister's husband and she were sound asleep. It least that was the way it appeared. He put a shot into her husband's head and another in his chest. As he was about to close the door, she turned her head. Their eyes locked extremely briefly, and Life shot out of the room. His exit was going to be clean anyway, but he was more than surprised to hear not a single stir as he made his way out of the basement window.

Once home, Life paid George Cornwell the other grand, and told him that his life depended on his keeping quiet. He knew he'd have no problem with George. George liked doing favors for him, and he was well versed enough in computers to perform the tasks Life needed to establish an alibi if necessary. Life covered George in the back of his second vehicle, drove him to the east side, and cut him loose.

A month went by. The murders were major league news, but nobody had yet approached Life. He was at his restaurant preparing the menu he was going to serve at his food stand at Indiana Black Expo, when one of the busboys told him that there was someone waiting for him in the dining room. "Cops," was the first thing he thought. But even if they'd found his DNA at the scene, it could be easily explained away by his relationship with Meena – his dear, soulful Meena. He hated to admit it, but sentimental value wasn't the only reason why he'd kept one photo of them together.

He took a deep breath when he saw Meena's sister. She half smiled back at him, seated at the same table where they'd met before. He walked over and sat across from her. "I'm sorry to hear about your parents," said, sounding very sincere.

"Thank you," she returned, sadly.

"What can I do for you?"

She sighed, and slid a diary across the table to him. "Meena loved you very much," she said.

"I know."

"Things are changing at the compound."

"How so?"

"Let's just say that people will have the freedom to pursue their dreams."

"But they'll still keep a balance of faith?"

"Meena would have it no other way."

"I take it you're running things now," Life asked.

"There's going to be a fight, but I'm here, and they're over there."

"I'll help you any way that I can, within reason."

"I already know. You can count on me calling on you. One of us might need a job."

"You've already got it."

Jassi got up to walk away. She hesitated, and turned to him. "Listen, I'm just going to be honest."

"Please do."

"Meena was willing to die for her love for you. You're obviously a very honorable man. I plan to be a widow for at least the next year, and then I'll be available to date. I think I want to try things the way Meena tried them. Would you know anyone who might be interested?"

"I know some very honorable men."

"I know you do," Jassi smiled, and she walked out of the restaurant.

25 Years

A Short Story

By

E. Marvin Neville

Dr. Courtney Kelly waited patiently for his two younger sisters at the Benihana Japanese restaurant at Keystone at the Crossing at the north side of Indy at Eighty-Sixth Street and Keystone Avenue. He didn't really care much for Benihana's, but he knew that his estranged sisters would find it to be a treat. Belinda and Maria were two and four years younger than he respectively. He hadn't seen much of either of them over the last fifteen years. He hated them both. It wasn't entirely their fault that he hated them. In fact, it was probably mostly not their fault that he hated them. After all, they were all merely children at the time. But still, he hated them. "Belinda and Maria," he thought. He used to call them BM for bowel movement. That made him smile.

Dr. Courtney Kelly, at a relatively young forty years of age, was one of the preeminent surgeons in the Midwest, with specialties in both heart and brain surgery. He'd written two books, authored countless articles, was a highly sought after public speaker, and had made extremely wise investments with his proceeds. He felt the sting of the 2008 economic collapse, but he was one of those fortunate individuals called upon by Barrack Obama to take on more of the tax burden. He was fortunate because he was clearly willing to pay more to make a better economic America. He didn't like the fact that his investments on Wall Street were doing better percentage wise than his wholly owned businesses. His medical product distribution center was doing better than even. It seemed that bad economic times equaled good economic times for hospitals and doctor's offices. People seemed to get sick more when there wasn't as much medical coverage for them. All told, Courtney was worth nearly forty million dollars. Dr. Courtney Kelly had become a huge success in life despite his horrific childhood. He married a White woman, had thirteen and ten year old daughters who were smart, gorgeous, and athletic like their mother who'd excelled in gymnastics in high school, and appeared to have adjusted well to being bi-racial. He wished often that his mother was still alive to see what he'd become.

BM strode into the Benihana's. As was expected by Courtney, Belinda seemed apprehensive while Maria appeared completely entitled. The duo was a far cry from the skinny, ashy, maple syrup colored girls who'd help their insane mother make Courtney's life such a horror. They were both overweight Black women, much like the majority of Central Indiana Black females. They looked ordinary, and they were. But there was a question as to which of them was more ordinary than the other.

Belinda had done okay in her life. Like Courtney, she'd always been focused on a medical profession. She'd become a Registered Nurse just over thirteen years ago. She had two children – one by each by her former and current husbands. Her family was just comfortable enough. They had struggles, but her son and daughter were decently adjusted, her husband maintained work as a forklift operator, and they owned their own home off of 62nd and Alton Avenue in Pike Township.

Maria, on the other hand, had been a ghetto bitch almost from the day she was born. She was the baby sister, and had gotten her way almost from her first draw of independent breath. She now had four children by three different fathers, lived mostly off of government assistance, and seemed to always need help of some kind. Belinda helped her when she could. Courtney never helped Maria financially, and hardly otherwise. He assisted Belinda every now and then, but she was required to repay him. She always repaid him. Even when she felt that she shouldn't have to repay her brother, she did anyway. She didn't want to be crushed emotionally and lawfully on Judge Judy. At least that was what she told herself.

Morty Spillman was a name that only Courtney, among the siblings, had thought about even fairly often in the last twenty five years. He was the man who'd confessed to the murder of their mother, Barbara Kelly. His life sentence had run out. He was dead of a heart attack. The Indianapolis DA had wanted additional child molestation charges attached to his conviction, but Courtney had refused to testify against Morty in 1983.

"Why couldn't we meet at your house, Courtney? Are you ashamed of us?" Maria asked snidely.

"Please stop, Maria," Belinda blurted. "We're getting a free meal at a restaurant I can't afford to look at, and that you can't afford to even think about.

"Funny, Belinda," Dr. Kelly responded.

"Well, she's right, Courtney. How do you think it makes us feel to know that you're cleaning out the bank, but you treat us and our families like the dog shit you stepped in while on your morning jog around Geist Reservoir," Maria said angrily.

"Good question, Maria. Let me ask you this? How do you think it made me feel when you two were letting Barbara beat the shit out of me for shit you did, or let her starve me while you were sleeping off the effects of fried chicken."

"We were just kids, Courtney," Belinda interjected. What did you want us to do?"

"Certainly a little more than nothing."

"That's not fair, Dr. Kelly," Maria emphasized his name sarcastically. "Momma was hard on us too."

"Yeah, that's right. She yelled at you when she found out that your eleven year old ass was fucking your sixteen year old boyfriend. And, by the way, where is he? Oh, that's right. After siring your first two children before you were twenty, and five other kids before he turned twenty-six, he beat a seventy-five year old White woman to death for twenty-seven dollars. He was really smart."

Maria leered at her brother. "You think you're better than me?" she asked from between clinched teeth.

"Do you really need me to answer that?"

"That's enough," Belinda admonished. "We know that you hate us, Courtney. Why did you ask us here?"

"Thank you, Belinda. As I'm sure you know, Morty Spillman died in prison yesterday."

"Yeah, well, he should've died in the electric chair twenty-five years ago for what he did to our mother," Maria offered.

"Maybe," Courtney returned. "But there's a story behind his death that I think you both deserve to know about."

"We know he molested you, Courtney. And that he killed mom when she caught him doing it at his store. Everybody knows that," Belinda said.

"Okay. Can I tell you anyway?"

"Might as well," Maria sneered. "It's gonna take me time to eat everything on the menu."

"Good," Courtney said. Both of his sisters sighed in unison. They would end up quite unpleasantly surprised.

The horrors started for Courtney only a few weeks after their father, Matt Kelly, walked away from his family. In fact, he ran. And once Courtney got his first taste of Barbara Kelly's true personality, he could see why his father dashed for the hills. The woman was simply crazy.

Courtney's major misfortune was easy to identify. He was a victim of Matt's genetic code. By the time he was eight years old he'd so tired of people claiming that there was no way that his father could even consider denying him as his son that he started saving part of his meager allowance for cosmetic surgery. But he truly loved his dad. He'd never been a momma's boy. It didn't matter. Every time Barbara looked at her only son, she saw the only man she'd ever loved and hated. But as crazy as she was, she and stupidity were separated by light years.

Courtney, Belinda, and Maria rarely saw their father, but he himself went to court to insure the support of his children. Courtney saw as much of that support as an earthworm saw life after stranding itself on a sidewalk in the hot sun. The one thing good thing that Courtney had gotten from Barbara was a healthy love of health care. She was a nurse practitioner, so she made a decent living without the child support. But for Courtney, her finances translated into very little. While the girls got new clothes almost monthly, he mostly got hand me downs from people he knew. The humiliation of wearing a garment that had been previously owned by an acquaintance and/ or a classmate, and to have that individual see him wearing it often drove him to want to commit suicide. When Belinda and Maria got smothered pork chops for dinner, he got a bowl of Cheerios. When they got pancakes for breakfast, he got Cap'n Crunch. He loved Cap'n Crunch, but still. When Courtney's sisters misbehaved, they got the requisite spankings, groundings, and restrictions. Barbara Kelly once slapped him so hard across the face that a tooth flew out of his mouth and fell down the kitchen sink because he'd corrected her about the calendar date of that day. Courtney decided by the age of nine that once he became old enough and strong enough, he was going to kill her with his bare hands. He would choke her to death, or beat her to death, or both. And then he would stab her so that her soul would flow like a bursting dam into hell. At nine years old, he figured the death penalty was worth it. After all, he'd been wishing he was dead since a few weeks after Matt Kelly had left the family. But then, something very unusual happened.

By the age of thirteen, Courtney's beatings had diminished markedly. He was stronger, and Barbara was finding it increasingly more difficult to keep him from escaping her clutches. The best that she could do really was to keep his room free of the accoutrements of even the poorest of teenagers short of homelessness. His room was basically a 1981 prison cell. Barbara wanted to give his room to Maria, and have him sleep on the living room sofa, but her terrorizing of him had retarded his growing out of wetting the bed. She forced him to clean up his messes, but his room smelled like a bus station men's room.

"Yeah, I remember the kids all calling you pee boy," Maria recalled laughing.

"Yeah, I remember that neither of you ever came to my defense."

"We were kids, Courtney," Belinda sighed.

"You were sixteen, Belinda. You never even tried to comfort me. But I give you props. Unlike your ho of a sister, at least you never teased me."

"You know, Courtney, I'm not scared to grab one of these knives, jump across this table and stab your ass," Maria threatened.

"I know you're not, and I welcome you to try. I mean, let's face it. You had a fight with Barbara when you were nine years old because she wouldn't let you go visit your thirteen year old boyfriend. I'm mean, what thirteen year old boy wants to fuck a nine year old girl unless he's a pedophile? And what nine year old girl wants to fuck any boy unless she's a ho in training?"

"Guys, we're going to get thrown out of here if you don't quiet down," Belinda sighed, and then she looked at Courtney. "What's the point of this?"

Courtney explained the point to his more responsible, more level-headed sister. After the argument between Barbara and Maria, he knew what to expect. By the next morning, Maria would be assessed a punishment of what amounted to a slap from a pinky finger on her wrist, whereas he might well be hit with a baseball bat. He wanted nothing to do with that night. He climbed out of his bedroom window. He figured that Barbara would drink herself to sleep that night, and he'd be able to beat her in a physical fight the next day. Hell, maybe he'd follow through with his killing fantasies. He'd be on the streets by his twenty-first birthday, and, given his mother's abuse of him, maybe before his eighteenth. He was only a few blocks away from home when he saw the lights on at the neighborhood variety store. It was the Star Variety Store, and it was owned and operated by Morty Spillman.

Morty Spillman was a forty-five year old Jewish widower whose wife had been unable to bear children. She'd died under mysterious circumstances in 1975, but nothing could be attached to Morty, or anyone else by Indianapolis authorities, so he ended up with a beautiful home in Meridian Hills, substantial life insurance proceeds, and money that she'd brought into the marriage. He could afford to keep a tiny variety store in a Black neighborhood where there was probably more thieving than there was purchasing. That was exactly why Courtney

Kelly decided to enter Star Variety Store on that particular night. He was hungry, and he was broke.

It was 1981. Indianapolis was eons away from the hot, jumping, tourism and convention magnate it had become by 2008. Robert Irsay, the late owner of the Indianapolis Colts reportedly exclaimed in 1984 as he seriously considered moving the franchise from Baltimore because of the freshly built Hoosier Dome that "he stood on Illinois Street on a Saturday evening in downtown and could've shot a cannonball down the street and nobody would've noticed." In 1981, there were still a few neighborhood variety stores. But there were not the Speedway Starvin' Marvin type gas station/ convenience stores where a person could literally buy a three course meal while gassing up. Courtney's food options were limited. But a couple of Snicker's candy bars and a bag of potato chips wouldn't be bad. He slipped into the store, and nodded to Morty. He walked about the store more concerned about whether or not Morty was watching him than about the fact that his mother would kill him if she found out that he wasn't home. The store was empty except for the two of them which, even at the tender age of thirteen, Courtney knew wasn't the best circumstance for theft. But he was hungry. He fingered a few different bars before picking up a large Snicker's. He dropped it to the floor after feeling a hand on his right shoulder. It was Morty Spillman, who was obviously part snake. "I've seen you around here for years, kid. You've never stolen from me before. Why are you stealing from me now?"

"I ain't stealing," Courtney exclaimed.

"You're not now, But that's only because I caught you."

Courtney started to walk away, but Morty stopped him. "Look, I know you're hungry, man," Morty said kindly.

"How would you know that?" Courtney snapped defensively.

"I could hear your stomach growling from behind the counter, that's how. Look, I've got some food in the back. If you want, I'll take care of you. You just have to make sure that it's our secret."

"Why's that?"

"I don't want every hungry kid in the neighborhood strolling in here trying to steal something so that I'll feed them," Morty laughed. "Why don't you go on to the back. I've got some food on a little stove back there. You can have dinner with me."

Courtney was hesitant, but the emptiness of his stomach combined with the divine aroma emanating from the back room drew him to slowly make his way back there. Morty closed and locked up the store, and proceeded to feed Courtney. He told the boy what the food was, but Courtney barely heard him. He had no idea how good the food truly was because he was hungry enough to eat an elephant's hide. In time, Courtney would become an expert in Jewish cuisine, impressing even Jews. But Morty Spillman gave him much more in the two years before Barbara Kelly's death, and Morty's subsequent incarceration.

Morty was a highly educated man, whose parents had wanted him to become a doctor. But Morty was more inclined toward business, more accurately, to legally hustle. He'd started and had had a number of small businesses fail in his life. But by the time he married his late wife, a furrier heiress, he had only two that he stuck, a kosher deli in Nora and the Star Variety Store near Haughville. His wife died in 1978, and he inherited her multi-millions. He sold the deli, but he kept the variety store. He needed the variety store.

Morty was even tempered, and a great communicator. He turned out to be more than a father figure for Courtney. He was an extraordinary mentor. Morty calmed Courtney's anger, and taught him how to avoid his mother's ire by delving into a world of high academia, and preparing himself for his own future. Before long, Courtney didn't care what his mother did to him, didn't do for him, or even what her drunken ass thought of him. His grades exploded past Belinda's, who'd always been good in school, and he even saw his mother thrusting more anger toward Maria, who'd always been good at trying to get a dick inside of her as soon as humanly possible. Courtney was able to remain mostly neglected and alone in his room at home to study, while Barbara spent increasingly more time arguing with Maria about her boy craziness. But mostly he cherished his time with Morty. Morty taught him compassion, concern, consideration, and focus. Morty literally made him into the success that he'd become. But Morty had done so by being far more, or far less, than a father figure.

It was a cool Friday afternoon in Indy. School would be out for Fall Break the following week, and Courtney looked forward to spending the lion's share of that break with Morty. Things went as usual that afternoon. They completed all of Courtney's assigned homework for the vacation week, he ate a fine home-cooked meal, and Morty gave him a paper sack of food to sneak home and eat later. And then, something changed. Morty seemed sad.

"What's wrong, Morty," the thirteen year old asked concerned.

Morty sighed. "Well, I don't feel well," he said softly.

"Is there something I can do to help?"

"I don't think so, son. I'm going to close up early and go home."

"Are you sure there's nothing I can do?"

Morty looked pensively at Courtney. "Do you trust me?" he asked.

"Of course I do. You're all I really have."

Morty sighed again. He looked up at Courtney. "Can you keep a secret?" he asked, his voice trembling.

"Yes," Courtney answered as confidently as he could, given the fact that he was mortified.

"What I'm about to show you might make you uncomfortable. In fact, it will make you uncomfortable. But I need for you to understand that it's truly very, very natural. Dou you understand, Courtney?"

Courtney nodded yes, and with that, Morty dropped to his knees between Courtney's legs, unzipped Courtney's jeans, reached inside, and freed Courtney's penis. With quivering hands, he fumbled it into his mouth. It sprang to stiffness, and Morty loved it as if it were owned by a Greek god. Courtney wasn't sure what to do or what to think, so he simply succumbed. Within minutes, Morty grunted and shook with his orgasm. He kept going until Courtney ejaculated only a few minutes later. Beyond wet dreams, it was Courtney's first, and his very first orgasm. It tickled. It felt good.

Both Courtney and Morty were silent as Morty let him out of the store. Courtney was confused. But, oddly, he wasn't scared. He had yet to even kiss a girl, without tongue even, and he'd already come inside of the mouth of another human being. The first year of their relationship, Courtney was the consummate student. Not that he'd ever been less than an average student in school, but in 1981, he began to see the work clearly – even in classes he didn't like. But he also became the ultimate male to male lover. The first time Morty gently penetrated him anally, he pissed his pants thinking he was about to ejaculate. He nearly puked the first time he took Morty in his mouth. But Morty was caring and patient, telling to only work the head. Courtney was a natural, however. It wasn't long before he could take a pounding on his face and his ass. He came to love the smell of a man's inner thighs, and the feel of a throbbing penis in his mouth.

By 1982, the tables were well turned. Courtney was screwing Morty daily and well. At times, he literally had to beg Morty to blow or sodomize him. Morty not only threw money at him, he completely set up Courtney's college fund.

"We knew you got molested, Courtney, but we didn't know you liked it," Maria said as she chomped on a lobster tail as if it were a chicken drumstick.

Belinda shook her head. She'd barely touched her food. "How can you be gay? I mean, you have a wife and two kids," she lamented.

"That's right," Maria spouted, lobster bits sprayed out of her mouth. "Maybe I should tell her. That would be worth maybe ten grand."

"It would be worth more than that, Maria. But let me finish my story before you decide whether or not you want to blackmail me." He looked at Belinda. "You see, my dear sisters, I'm not really gay. Not in the homosexual sense of the term."

Belinda exploded from her seat. "I don't want to hear any more of this," she exclaimed.

Courtney leered at her. "You owe me this," he said.

She sat down slowly, looking down at her nearly full plate of food.

Courtney proceeded to explain to his sisters that he loved women. Even at his most confusing time between his relationship with Morty, and his awkwardness with girls, he never stopped loving girls. He did well with them, in fact. He contributed some of his success with girls to what he learned through his relationship with Morty. But he knew that it was mostly because he had money. He'd never been more than an average-looking guy, but he was smart, savvy, and he had cash. Morty had seen to that. But Courtney never flashed. He merely made sure that he always had enough cash to cover meager expenses. Only he, Morty, and The Bank of Indianapolis were privy to the funding.

But Courtney never fought his desire to be with men. In high school, it was the most difficult. He wasn't gay, and he didn't want to be labeled as such because the consequences would be dire, and he might well have found himself fighting daily. The sneaking around, and hiding in the shadows was almost as devastating as when his teenaged gay lovers wanted exclusive relationships with him.

The college years were a considerably easier. Courtney attended UCLA's pre-med program. He wanted to get as far from Indy as he could. The freedom and more tolerant attitude of Southern California in the late eighties were very welcome for him. Still, he never advertised his homosexual activities. He maintained meaningful relationships with three women, and had meaningless sex with at least a dozen others during his time on the Westwood campus. But, as he continued to keep his homosexual activities hidden, he realized something quite profound.

By the time he started medical school at IUPUI back in Indy, Courtney came to realize that not only did a hidden sexual culture exist, but that he'd become a member of it without really even knowing. It was the down low culture, and Courtney figured that he might well have been one of the founding fathers. A class of professional men with families grew through the 1990's, and thrived like a coca plant in a South American rain forest. That class of men had sex with other men. They usually kept to themselves, or in small groups. Courtney claimed to have a lover that he was going to see as soon as he left the restaurant. He was fourth generation Chinese and a medical student with a future brighter than the sun. "I like them young, but not as young as I was," Courtney said. "They have to be eighteen or older."

"God, you're a sick, nasty bastard," Maria groaned.

"Did Aunt Regina or Uncle Phil know? I mean, you know, did they know after they took us in?" Belinda asked.

"If they did they never breathed a word to me. I'm sure they didn't know," Courtney responded.

"You know, maybe this motherfucker drugged our food and plans to take us someplace and do freaky shit to us," Maria said.

"Maria, even if you weren't my sister I wouldn't give a skank like you a second look if you walked up to me in a dark alley and showed me your swamp of a pussy."

"I'll fucking jump across this table and stab you with a steak knife."

"The problem is you'll never even make it halfway before I slam your face through the table. In fact, your face would probably never touch the table since your ugliness is like a Star Trek force field."

"That's enough, you two," Belinda interrupted knowing that they were beginning to attract attention to the table.

"Well, look-y-here. You finally step up to the plate," Courtney smiled.

"Fuck you, Courtney," Belinda said quietly. "Why are we here?"

"I'll tell you why we're here, sister," Maria said. "We're here because this asshole finally wants to apologize to us for getting momma killed."

"That's the smartest thing you've said so far, Maria. Too bad it's not true," Courtney said.

Belinda's lips began to quiver. She stared at her brother. "You killed momma, didn't you?" she asked.

Courtney nodded his head, and gritted his teeth. "I wanted Barbara dead, Belinda. I'll admit that. But I didn't kill her. Morty helped to appreciate life. He's the main reason I became a doctor," he said.

"So Morty Spillman did kill momma."

"Unfortunately for Morty, he probably thought I killed her. That's the only reason that I can think of that he ended up being convicted. I mean, after all, blaming me might have helped him. On the other hand, he would've exposed himself to being a child molester. It didn't matter that the true molestation had dissolved after the first time he slipped his mouth over my dick."

"Again, Courtney, why are we here?" Belinda asked angrily, but quietly.

"Do you remember anything else about that day, Belinda?"

"I don't know, Courtney. That was twenty-five years ago."

"How about you, Maria?" he asked.

"I'm getting tired of you, man."

"Okay then. I'll go. Maybe you two remember that the middle school called. They said that they caught Maria damn near fucking a sixteen-year old boy in a stairwell. I believe his name was Derrick."

"So what," Maria scoffed.

"When Morty realized that Barbara had followed me to the store, he panicked. He hustled me out the back door and told me to wait there until he told me to leave. But he never got the chance to do that. I heard him and Barbara screaming at each other through the locked front door. But I couldn't help myself. I started up the alley toward the front of the store to see the confrontation. Imagine my surprise when I saw somebody running up behind Barbara. Imagine, again, my surprise when I heard momma screaming that it was a shameful embarrassment than an eleven-year old girl was pregnant."

Belinda looked at her baby sister, tears streaming from her eyes. "YOU Killed momma?"

"No I didn't," Maria responded.

"You stabbed her three times, Maria. You murdered her with that butcher knife that Barbara used to use to cut food and tenderize meat. You know the one I'm talking about, don't you Belinda – the one with the cherry wood handle that came up missing? It was the only one like it in the drawer. I think she said several times that it had been passed down from her great-great-great-great grandmother who'd used it to carve up animals that they'd tricked their owners into thinking were sick by clubbing them on the head with whatever they could find that was sufficiently heavy. Did you ever see that knife again, Belinda? I didn't. Where'd you hide the knife, Maria?"

"I don't know what the fuck you're talking about, Courtney," Maria said indignantly.

"Sure you do," Courtney said as he reached into a satchel on the floor beside him that, until then, neither of the sisters had seen. In a large freezer bag was a girl's top covered with blood. "Remember this?" he asked.

Belinda gasped, holding back the vomit building in her gut. She recognized the top. It had been Maria's favorite until their mother's murder. It had a silkscreen of Janet Jackson on the front. "YOU killed momma?"

"She said she was going to report Derrick to the police!" Maria exclaimed.

"The school had already done that," Courtney offered.

"She was going to put up posters saying that he was a rapist. He wasn't."

"According to the law, he was," Courtney said. He threw the baggie across the table to Maria. "Don't you ever in your life even think that I've never done anything for you, Maria? I let you get away for twenty-five years with murdering the one person in my life who showed me love." Courtney got up from the table. "I've set up college funds for both of your children, Belinda, and for your youngest two, Maria. Maybe they'll turn out to be better citizens than their parents."

"We were just children, Courtney," Belinda cried

"I know. So was the eleven-year old who murdered your mother," he answered as he headed for the door.

"Courtney," Belinda called out. He stopped, and turned toward them. Belinda was truly saddened, while Maria seemed angry. "Why didn't you stop Morty from going to prison?" Belinda asked.

Courtney smiled. "Are you kidding? Belinda, the man was a pedophile."

A Triangle Of Perfection

A Short Story

By

E. Marvin Neville

Wade Robinson was as terrified as a kitten cornered by a pit bull as he stumbled back into his swanky home. He'd never been religious, but always spiritual. He'd believed in reincarnation from the age of twelve. But other than dreams and happenings that had multitudes of explanations, he'd never experienced anything like he'd experienced only a few minutes ago. He'd soiled himself. He hadn't done that since he was an infant.

Wade was an orphan. His parents had been shot to death in a drug deal gone crazy in 1971, so he'd never known them. He was only three. He'd started writing stupid poems at age eight, but he'd fallen in love with writing even before he'd even written the first stupid poem. Reading had been his lifeline. It was the only thing he loved more than writing, and that was only because it required less work. He was lucky, though. He was a Black kid who was adopted by a White woman who loved a Black when Wade was five. His adoptive parents never married. They were afraid that Wade would be taken away from them. At that time, their bi-racial adoption was as about as popular as a Black man being Grand Dragon of the KKK. He was even luckier that the couple agreed to teach him both European and African cultures patiently, and they were lucky that he was too bright to become angry because of the hugely diverse teachings. He was great looking, and greatly focused. He just wanted to write. He had something to say, and he was determined to not only write what he had to say, but he wanted to make absolutely certain that what he had to say was important enough for the world to want to hear it.

Wade breezed through school. He graduated from Northwestern University in Evanston, IL with a 3.2 GPA in Journalism with a minor in Business Management. He'd always wanted to write, understand, and control his writing career, with minimal assistance by managers and agents.

Wade met Rhonda Carlson his junior year at Northwestern. She was closing in on a nursing degree. He never understood why anybody would come to such a prestigious university to become a nurse, but, after spending time with her, he learned quickly. Nurses from Northwestern had a much better chance of becoming doctors than nurses from Ivy Tech. They hit it off like hot butter sauce over a lobster tail. They were from different worlds, but they tasted oh so good together.

Rhonda had come from a working class family of five children, and her education had been funded by meager scholarships, slim parental funding, and massive student loans. She hailed from Chicago, so she was able to stay at home. She hated that, but she never let anyone know how much until she met Wade at an Omega Psi Phi party. She'd been drunk, and he'd fostered there before. They were both so incredibly smart and so incredibly focused, they clicked immediately. She became pregnant only because she'd simply forgotten to ingest her birth control pill, and they'd long ago passed the condom stage. Rhonda was showing on graduation day.

Wade took a job at The Indianapolis Star as a cub reporter, while Rhonda worked as a nurse. They married in front of a judge with the twins in attendance after Rhonda graduated from nursing school. Her getting a job as a nurse looked good for their forging future, but something else happened that brightened their future exponentially.

Wade found a niche for himself in the microscopic world of commercial writing. He produced brochures, sales letters, instruction manuals and such. By his thirtieth birthday, he was making three-hundred thousand dollars per year from his job and his business. It wasn't long before he became a work at home husband. It was good. He was with the twins a great deal more than he might have been as an investigative reporter, he didn't have to actually go to work daily, and he was the parent who dominated the home. Plus, he was able to afford private school for the twins. They responded spectacularly – excelling in school, and developing into fine citizens. But the Bill Cosby-like family existence had cracks that Wade realized, too late, that he'd ignored for a long time.

As the financial manager for the family, Wade recognized a strange pattern. Rhonda was working overtime that wasn't showing up on her paychecks. He'd chosen to ignore the discrepancy for a while, but, eventually, his curiosity overcame his fear. He drove up to the parking structure between Capitol and Hall streets directly across from Methodist Hospital where Rhonda worked and caught her screwing a surgical intern in the car that he was paying for. She couldn't talk him out of divorce. He sacrificed half of his earnings, and took up residence in a modest apartment less than a mile from the home to make sure that his children were very well taken care of. The divorce decree covered all issues.

Seven years after the divorce, the twins were eighteen-years old, and off to college. Wade had bolstered their college funds with five additional months of support payments, giving the twins twenty-five thousand dollars each to use in college as they needed. He was also off the hook for the fourteen-hundred dollar per month mortgage he'd agreed to pay to keep Rhonda and the twins living in the way they'd always known. But that wasn't even close to the best of what happened to him.

A woman Wade was dating found and read journals he'd kept chronicling how difficult it had been to maintain his family from less than a mile away for eleven thousand four hundred dollars per month. He got along famously with his twin son and daughter, but it took a great deal of effort, and he'd fallen into doing little more than running his business and keeping his journal. His girlfriend's finding and reading of the journal caused their breakup, but she turned out to be absolutely correct in convincing him to turn the journals into a book. Knowing the difficulty in convincing one of the big New York publishing houses to publish a first-time author, Wade published "The Pain of Divorce" with Author House, a vanity publisher from nearby Bloomington, Indiana. Fifty-thousand were sold in Central Indiana alone. Knopf, a New York publishing giant, took notice. They proffered Wade Robinson a five-hundred thousand dollar advance that was quickly covered by explosive sales. By the time Wade returned home from a six-month publicity tour for "The Pain of Divorce", he was a millionaire with millions more in income glowing in his future.

The first order of business for America's newest millionaire was to increase everything regarding his living conditions. He wanted to live downtown, with a view of the Indianapolis skyline. He checked around Lockerbie Square and Chatham Arch but those homes were too small. The Old Northside had homes with space, but none that had a skyline view were available. And then his real estate agent took him to the Watermark Housing development. It was about thirty luxurious homes in the block between Senate Ave. and the downtown canal, and Walnut and North Streets. Not only did the house being sold have a spectacular view of the skyline, it was also on the canal. He paid cash.

It was a sweltering day in Indy. It was the part of summer between the fourth of July, and Labor Day. Wade had just moved in his last piece of furniture – a pool table for the basement and canal level of his new home. Rhonda called his cell. She was nearby and wanted to pop in to see his new home. She was amazed at his taste in décor. He'd furnished his home in earth tones and all African art. They both took seats on the sofa.

"This is really nice," Rhonda said.

"Thanks. Would you like something to drink, or something?"

"Or something."

"Excuse me?" Wade asked.

"It's been a while since we've been together, Wade. I thought we'd christen your new house, unless you've done that already."

"Well, I'm not seeing anybody right now. I'm too busy. What about your boyfriend?"

"I don't have one, but that never stopped you before."

"That was over four years ago, Rhonda."

"Look. I know I did you wrong. But I don't think I ever really stopped loving you."

"Well, it took a long time, but I can't say the same."

"Does that mean we don't christen the house?"

It didn't. They made love on his bed and later on his brand new pool table that had yet to even see a pool ball. They lay breathlessly upon it. "Wow. That was as great as ever," Rhonda said.

"Yes it was," Wade answered.

"Listen. Will you hear me out on something?"

"I'm listening."

"What if I were to sell my house, and move in here with you?"

"I don't understand."

"Well, before I screwed up, I thought we had it pretty good," Rhonda said.

"So did I."

"Well, the kids will be off to college in a few weeks. Maybe we can make another go of it."

Wade rolled off of the table. He looked for his underwear, but remembered that he'd left them in the bedroom, so he stood there naked. "You've had seven years to get ready for this, Rhonda," he said.

"What're you talking about?"

"You can't make the payments on the house, can you?"

"What do house payments have to do with anything?"

"Come on, Rhonda. You don't love me. You love my new found wealth."

"I can't believe you said that."

"Okay. Answer me truthfully, and if I'm wrong, I'll not only apologize, I'll give your proposal serious consideration."

"Okay, Wade. I'm a month behind. I can't handle fourteen-hundred dollars a month. But that's not why I want to move in with you. I really want to give us a try again."

"You know. It's funny. In those early years after our divorce when we slept together, you never made mention of ever wanting to get back together."

"I was ashamed, Wade."

Wade shook his head. "Well, I can't go for it again. But I'll tell what I will do. I'll pay the mortgage completely off, but it's a buyout, not a gift."

"What do you mean?"

"I'll own the house."

"So you can throw me out whenever you want."

"You know me better than that. Maybe if you weren't the mother of my children I'd consider it. But I'm not that kind of man."

"That's not fair, Wade."

"I don't see how I could be more fair, Rhonda. Now please get dressed and leave."

Rhonda reluctantly agreed to the deal, and left.

Other than the twins, the only other good thing that Wade got from Rhonda was the ability to cook. She taught him the basics, and he took it from there once he was on his own. He bought several cookbooks so that he would spend as little as possible on takeout. A cooking man was good for dating, and when he'd had time to date, he'd often cooked his way right into his date's panties. Now he could afford to hire a chef. But, still, he preferred to prepare his own meals. It didn't take long for the word to get around the Watermark that when Wade fired up his grill on the terrace overlooking the canal, the other waterfront residents should open up their terrace windows. The smells were phenomenal, and he sent them out there almost every weekend while he worked on his second novel. Those aromas put him into the position of meeting the women who would change his life.

Two twenty-one year old women lived in the apartment almost exactly the across the canal from his grilling terrace. They'd often come out onto their balcony and made motions as if they were waving the aroma into their apartment. He'd thought about inviting them over, but he didn't think two young White girls would want to have anything to do with a Black divorcee who was careening wildly toward middle age. He'd smile and wave. He was happily astounded when they showed up at his basement level gate. Both girls were tall, slender, and athletic. One was blond the other had short, curly auburn hair. They were in their jogging outfits. Wade met them at his gate. "May I help you?" he asked.

The blond reached into a small bag she had around her waist. From it, she removed a book and turned the back photo to him. "Is this you?" she asked. "I say it is, but my roommate disagrees."

Wade took the book. "You got a pen?"

""See, I told you," the blond shouted excited. She handed Wade a pen from her bag. "I'm Sara McKenzie, and this is my best friend Lindsey Worthington."

"Well I guess you already know who I am, and I assume that since you handed me the book I'm making this out to you."

"Please make it out to both of us," Lindsey said. Sara nodded excitedly.

"Would you guys like to come in – have a beer or something?"

We'd love to," Sara said. She seemed to be the more outgoing of the two.

Wade gave Sara and Lindsey the full tour of the house as the two of them sipped on imported beers. Then the three of them took seats in his living room. He couldn't help but to notice how close the girls sat on the sofa. "Well, tell me something about yourselves ladies?"

Sara couldn't wait to speak up. "Well, we've known each other since the first grade. My dad's lawyer and hers is a businessman. We grew up in Geist, went to Park Tudor high school…."

"….Where we were teammates on three straight state tennis championship teams," Lindsey interrupted proudly.

"That's right. And now we're both pre-med at IUPUI. We both want to go into a pediatrics practice together," Sara added.

"What about boyfriends?"

"Who has time? Besides, they just get jealous when you spend more time studying than fawning over them," Sara answered. She had the biggest, brightest, bluest eyes he'd ever seen. They seemed to dance with happiness and confidence. Lindsey's eyes were brown, and not as large, but they seemed to know something.

"Listen, I was going to go out for Chinese," Wade said.

"Oh, we're so sorry. We can leave," Sara exclaimed.

No, no, no. I've got some chicken breasts in the fridge. I can whip that up along with some steamed vegetables and russet potatoes. We'll be eating in an hour. The girls looked at each other. Lindsey nodded excitedly. "I guess we'll get to see how well you cook inside the house," Sara smiled at him, and a very unusual friendship was born.

Over the next few weeks, the odd trio spent increasingly more time together. He cooked for them constantly, and they all jogged together almost daily. The girls loved watching movies on his seventy inch flat screen TV. Occasionally, they would bring over other girlfriends, or members of their sorority. To say that there weren't sometimes twinges of attraction between Sara, Lindsey, and Wade would be saying that they were inhuman. But such twinges were like swatting a moth from one's face. The erratic nature of them was bothersome, but they were easily swept aside.

After a jog one warm Friday night, the girls insisted that Wade accompany them to a nearby bar for Karaoke night. Lindsey loved to sing even though she wasn't very good. Sara convinced Wade to sing. He'd sung lead in his church choir when his parents had made him attend church. He knocked the bar dead. That night, he'd felt such camaraderie with them that he just slipped into calling Sara Mac. She liked it.

Mac and Lindsey had never even been within three football fields of a Black Expo event in downtown Indy. Word among those in their world was that it was owned by Black people, and that it was best for White's to stay away. Only one of those things was true.

Sunday night was the free concert at the American Legion Mall. It wasn't to start until seven in the evening, but Wade always got there no later than three in the afternoon to make sure that he got a decent seat. He, Mac, and Lindsey found a fabulous spot off of Pennsylvania and North streets. Wade had grilled enough chicken wings and bought enough liquor and beer to supply a team of Navy Seals. Some among the sea of Blackness around them looked at them as if he were pimping Mac and Lindsey. Several brothers even tried to step in as if they knew Wade to get closer to the girls, but were easily ignored. One guy didn't quite get the picture.

"Dude, no disrespect intended, but we don't know you. You're making my friends nervous, and we'd appreciate it if you'd either leave or stop trying to hit on them," Wade finally spoke up.

"These ladies look grown to me. I think it's up to them," the strange returned.

Then one of the men among a group on their left spoke up: "I'm sure they want you to go, man."

"Yeah, and you're standing in my way," a female voice rang out from behind.

"Fuck all you niggas," the man said as he strode away. There was a small cheer among those in the section. Wade passed out beers, and poured drinks.

A great time was had by all, and the trio struggled through sheer drunkenness to get their gear back to Wade's house. Everybody was tired, and sweaty. "You guys can stay here tonight," he offered.

"No, no. There's no way we're inconveniencing you," Lindsey slurred.

"Inconvenience me? It'll only take a few minutes for me to fix up the guest room."

"Are you sure?" Mac asked

"Well, I'd rather do that than have to walk you chicks home."

Lindsey laughed like a drunken sailor. It was settled.

Wade wasn't quite sleepy, so he decided to start journalizing his experiences with Mac and Lindsey. He'd wake up in the morning, realize that he'd written something in a drunken language, and tear the pages out. There was a gentle knock at the door. He wasn't sure whether or not he was hallucinating, so he said "come in" just to make sure. His door cracked open, and Mac's head slipped in. "Are you busy?" she asked.

"No, Mac. Do you need something? I know you know where everything is in the kitchen."

"I'm not hungry."

"Is there something wrong in the bedroom?"

"Yes. It keeps spinning."

"Well, I'll come out there with you."

"No, no, you're busy," Mac said.

"Please. I'm journaling our time together knowing full well that I won't understand a word I've written in the morning."

"Yours, mine, and Lindsey's relationship is something to write about, isn't it?"

"Yes," Wade answered. There was an awkward silence.

"Can I come in?"

"Sure, baby."

"Cool," Mac said as she entered Wade's bedroom, and sat on the far edge of the bed. "I had a lot of fun tonight."

"We all had a lot of fun."

"I've got to be honest. Lindsey and I were scared at first. And then that guy just invited himself to our party."

"Yeah, well, I've got to be honest, too. I was scared while he was there."

"Yeah, but you stood up anyway. And you didn't know that the strangers around us would back us up, did you?"

"No, I didn't."

Mac extended her arms for a friendly hug. She gave him a peck on the cheek. When she pulled her face away, their eyes met. She'd never looked so incredible, bloodshot eyes and all. Their mouths met in a hard, drunken kiss. Wade broke away. Mac got up. "I'm so sorry, Wade. I'd better go."

"No, Mac, it's not that I want you to go. It's just that, well, you and Lindsey are lesbians."

Mac looked at him as if he'd just sat up in a coffin. "How did you know that?"

"Well, baby, the way you two look at each other, especially when you're laughing. And you touch one another in a friendly way that shrouds intimacy – a gentle shoulder pat here, a deft thigh touch there. It's obvious that you love each other very much."

"Wow. I can't believe we're that obvious."

Wade smiled. "You're only obvious to the acutely observant. Plus, I've never seen you two with guys in any meaningful way. I mean, I'm not a voyeur, but guys pass through your apartment like tolerated mosquitoes – at least in the living room – and neither of you has ever brought a guy over here."

Mac smiled slyly, "Touché, Mr. Robinson. We'd thought about bringing over the occasional guy for cover, but you were too much man for the room. They just would've taken the fun out of the party." She turned to leave the room. Wade grabed her wrist, and pulled her back onto the bed. Their faces were so close, and the sensuality was so intense, it seemed that they could feel heat from each other's eyes. They kissed as if they'd hungered for each other for a lifetime. The drunkenness melted away into pure animal passion. They made love as if they would both be dead immediately following the act.

They awoke in each other's arms the next morning. The drunkenness that had melted away so easily when they'd committed the act of forbidden love the night before had come back in the form of a massive hangover. Mac got up and went to the guest room. She returned a few seconds later, looking quite distraught. Lindsey was gone, and so were Mac's clothes.

Wade watched Mac as she made her way across the Walnut Street Bridge to the west bank of the canal. He'd given her a pair of sweat pants, a t-shirt, and a leather jacket he'd owned since before his divorce. Had she and the borrowed garments not been so clean and kempt, she would've looked like a bag lady without the bags.

When Mac walked into her and Lindsey's apartment, she was met with a barrage of her clothes, led by the ones Lindsey had taken from Wade's home. "I want you out yesterday," Lindsey screamed.

"What are you talking about?" Mac asked.

"There's no time for bullshit, Sara!"

"I'm sorry."

"Are you kidding me? We've loved each other since the sixth grade."

"True."

"What're you saying Sara – that you love Wade?"

Mac hesitates. "Yes. I love you, and I love Wade. But we've talked about this before, Lindsey."

"Yes we have. But I thought we finally had enough toys to cover those feelings."

"Toys are great, baby. But there's nothing like having the occasional toy actually be pumping with human blood."

Lindsey looked lovingly at her girlfriend of nine years. "Okay. So you'd rather be with him?"

"I don't know, baby. I just don't know. But don't you love his cooking?" Mac smiled.

"You already know the answer to that. The question is whether or not you still love my cooking."

"I'll always eat anything you serve up," Mac responded. The lovers kissed, and all seemed right with the world.

The next night, Lindsey showed up at Wade's front door. He decided that a deluge of apologies was his best bet. He thought that he'd already lost his two best friends whose combined ages barely eclipsed his own., in addition to them both being White bread. Lindsey stopped him. "May I come in?" she asked.

"You know better than that, Lindsey," Wade responded.

Lindsey swept past Wade, and seated herself on the sofa. She looked back at him as he closed the door.

They talked about everything except the incident that had happened two nights ago between him and Mac. "We've decided to try something," she said.

"Who's decided to try something?"

"Come on, Wade," Lindsey responded with the calmness of a successful gunslinger. "You fucked my girlfriend."

"Your girlfriend fucked me too."

"Yes she did. And she seems to think that if I fuck you, not only will I understand why she did it, I'll better understand why the three of us have become such close friends."

"I don't have a clue what she means."

Lindsey kissed him. Her kiss was sweet but fearful. Wade recognized almost immediately what to do. In his mind, it was abundantly clear that Mac was the lesbian who was really more bisexual, and Lindsey was the one who truly wanted to be in love with another woman, but still liked occasional male stimulation.

Wade put Lindsey on her back, as they undressed each other. He felt with his finger that she was more than moist enough to be penetrated, but he didn't. He manipulated every erogenous zone that he could think of without penetrating her vagina with his penis. Her face, neck, ears, and breasts were glistening with saliva from his mouth. His hands traveled her full body as if they hadn't touched a woman in twenty years. And then he made the move. He moved his mouth to her inner thighs, still using both hands to manipulate her breast nipples. He breathed hot breath onto her thighs, licking them lightly. She shuddered. He lightly licked around the sea surrounding her clitoris until she moaned heavily and ground her pelvis against his face, and then went in for the kill – making sure that he alternated between her labia and her clitoris. He didn't know why he took that route. He knew only that it felt like the right thing to do. Lindsey screamed as she orgasmed onto his face.

Over the next few weeks, Wade, Mac, and Lindsey made love every way but together at once. Mac screwed Wade about three times per week. She loved the missionary position. It worked best for her as long as her partner was able to alternate. Once Wade plunged into her, he stood ground while she pumped. When she stopped, he pumped. What made him the best male lover that she'd ever had was the fact that he knew when to stop his thrusting, and allowed hers. The alternation method brought her to all of the orgasms that she needed to make sure that she truly loved Lindsey. She never stopped loving Lindsey.

In the dozens of times that Lindsey had made love to Wade, he'd never penetrated her with his penis. He simply worked her body as if he were another woman, and alternated between labia and clitoris with the deftness of an ancient goddess from the island of Lesbos. The sexual agreement between the three seemed perfect. It turned out to be far from it.

It was a Wednesday night, about eight pm. The temperature was eighty-five degrees, and the humidity was almost thick enough to see. After their jog, Mac and Lindsey asked Wade if they could bring over a movie to watch. Of course, he said yes to his two best friends with benefits. The movie was Beaches with Bette Midler and Barbara Hershey. Wade was a man who had no problem with his feminine side, but he wasn't one to buy movies that were made for women. He loved Beaches, though.

At eleven pm, Wade turned the channel to Comedy Central. He had to have his nightly fix of The Daily Show and The Colbert Report. He hated the news, but he loved to watch the news and politics being truthfully and irreverently skewered. Mac and Lindsey loved it too. It was at the beginning of the Colbert Report that Wade noticed something. The girls were sitting right up against him on either side. That had never happened before. He told himself that they were crowding his arms, so he put them around the girls. They both snuggled up to him. Now, he was a pimp – with two lesbians no less. Life was weird, but good.

After The Colbert Report, Wade was about to pick up the remote from the coffee table. Mac stopped him, and planted a sweet kiss on his right cheek."

"What was that for?" he asked

"For being you," Mac answered.

Lindsey gently put her fingers to his jaw, and turned his face to her. She kissed him on the lips.

"I'm afraid to ask," Wade said.

"We love you," Lindsey said.

"I love you guys, too," he returned

"We know," Mac smiled. "But you have to admit that this thing is really weird."

"Weird? Sometimes it scares me so much that I can't sleep," he answered.

"We're scared, too, "Lindsey said. "You're the best man, no, the best person we've ever known. You accepted us into your home. You feed us. You go out of your way for us. At the Black Expo concert, you put your life on the line for us."

"Well, I don't know about all that."

"In our eyes, you did," Mac said with serious warmth.

"You never judged us, Wade. You just let us into your life, and you asked us for nothing." Lindsey offered.

"I don't know what to say."

"We know," Mac said.

"That's why we've decided that we want to be with you," Lindsey smiled.

"I don't know what that means," Wade said.

"Neither do we," Lindsey answered.

Before Wade could utter another nonsensical statement, Mac kissed him at the side of his mouth. Lindsey joined in from the other side. They both slipped forward enough so that all three tongues could kiss at the same time. None of them had ever been in such a sensual position.

How they ended up naked in Wade's bed was a blur that they cared as about as much as a hungry frog cared about the maggots of a fly it had eaten. Mac was getting penis while on top of Wade, and Lindsey was getting mouth with her back to Mac. The move wasn't sudden. It was as smooth as heated fudge being poured. Lindsey turned around so that she was facing Mac. Wade had to make adjustments with his tongue so that he could continue to reach Lindsey's important erogenous zones. It was quite a strain, but he managed. The girls looked at each other. Their gaze was loaded with more love than they'd ever felt for one another. They both leaned in. They started kissing. It was the perfect triangle.

Within minutes, all three orgasms had built up like three balloons being over filled with water. When the balloons burst, cries rang out. Mac and Lindsey screamed into each other's mouths as Wade screamed into Lindsey's uterus. The shared sensuality quickly went from ecstatic to scary. Mac and Lindsey bled into each others mouths as Mac bled onto Wade's dick, and Lindsey bled into his mouth. They couldn't break apart, and they had no idea why. The room shook hard. It was a severe earthquake. Everything along the walls crashed to the floor. But then something truly strange happened. The bed rose off the floor. Still, they couldn't disconnect. The bed rocked and swayed. The trio was terrified beyond belief, but still they couldn't break away from each other. The bed bucked wildly from at least four feet off the floor, and finally threw the trio apart. Mac and Lindsey slammed off of opposite walls as if they'd been tossed by bulls. They fell unconscious immediately. Wade hit the ceiling. The light and fan fixtures cracked his ribs. He dropped back onto the bed. Drawing a breath was like getting a Japanese woman to marry a Black non-celebrity who wasn't rich.

Wade scrambled to his feet. He checked Mac and Lindsey. They were breathing. He bolted from his bedroom, and went outside. All he could hear was crickets. There should've been car alarms going off, and his neighbors should've been as frantic as was he. He was enormously perplexed. He went back inside. The rest of his house was completely undisturbed. His scared factor exploded. He ran back up to his bedroom. The girls were gone. He ran to his sliding glass door and saw them sprinting over the Walnut Street bridge, dressing along the way. He looked at the destruction that was his bedroom, and passed out.

The following Sunday, Wade walked out of his house toward Walnut Street, his ribs still sore. He hadn't seen or heard from Mac or Lindsey since that terrifying night. Their apartment had been cleared out completely. Rhonda was waiting for him in her car. He climbed in.

"Are you going to join church today, Wade?" she asked

"I don't know, Rhonda. Just keep picking me up and we'll go from there."

Baby Sister

A Short Story

By

E. Marvin Neville

Simone Sullivan had driven past the house on West 12th Street dozens of times over the last twenty-five years. Her older half brother had grown up there. She'd had a lot of friends in her thirty-six years of life, but she knew every enemy she'd ever had better than she knew her own brother. It never seemed right. None of it ever seemed right. She remembered the first time she'd seen a photograph of him, on their grandmother's grand piano. The piano was like an elephant in a bird cage in the tiny living room of the tiny house at 25th and Colombia on the east side of Indianapolis. But their grandmother was nothing else if not strict about injecting culture into the family to the best of her ability.

Tyler Justice had been living in the house that Simone had been constantly driving past the last few weeks of summer 2008 in Indiana for over four years. Tyler had lived in Los Angeles, Atlanta, and even Chicago throughout his life. He had only a high school diploma, but he'd always worked, and worked hard, mostly in manufacturing and warehousing. But now he was dive bombing toward fifty years of age and living at home with his seventy-five year old mother, three of his five younger sisters, one of his younger brothers, and three of his sister's five children. He was all but emotionally crushed. His mother's eleven children were sired by five different fathers. Oddly, he was the only one of his siblings whose father had sired only him. Tyler had decided well before his teenage years that he didn't want children. He hated having to make sure that he was home well before dinner time, such that it was, to make sure that he got enough to eat. His mother did her best, but she loved fucking men just slightly more than she loved providing for her children. His siblings and he had learned to love and care for one another, but more than fairly occasionally, a late arriving teen would have to eat a bologna sandwich instead of a dinner of fried chicken.

Simone never felt any fault about the fact that she was separated from her beautiful brother in the photograph on top of their grandmother's crucially out of place grand piano, but she'd always felt an emptiness. She reached out for the first time at the tender age of six years. She badgered their father and grandmother nearly every day to meet the young man in the photographs. Simone and Tyler finally met in the summer of 1978.

It was a hot summer following a winter that had made national headlines. Tyler was visiting Indy from Chicago, where he was employed manufacturing aircraft parts for American Airlines, to escape the horrific memory of the winter of 1977, and to spend time with his family. Already he was being mirthfully teased by his child bearing siblings about his refusal to have children. He already had two nieces and a nephew by his eighteenth birthday. His oldest brother, the father of his niece and one nephew, had secured a twelve pack of beer and a fifth of vodka, and he and his older brothers were having a good old time getting high, when the phone rang. It was Tyler's father. He, Simone, and one of her very young friends were at a church revival in Haughville, and Simone was clamoring to see him. She knew that the house where he'd grown up was close by. Tyler was rolling up a joint at the time, but he felt compelled to meet his baby sister. He didn't know why. He just felt that he had to meet her. It seemed right.

Tyler was struck by his baby sister. She was, by far, the most beautiful six-year old person he'd ever seen. When their eyes met there was an instant connection, but it was buffered by the years of uncertainty placed there by their respective parents. Their dad allowed him to drive her and her friend home anyway. Simone was so shy with him, but he was able to get both she and her friend to laugh. She melted, and so did he. But Tyler had a life in Chicago at the time, and Simone was a little girl trapped in a family that just didn't feel right.

Simone Porter wanted love. It seemed like such a simple concept – people loving each other. But she learned by the time she was ten that love had levels. Her mom and dad, and even her step brother loved her. Her mom loved her because she wanted to have a child with her professionally drunken second husband in the hope that he would come to love her and their extended family more than he loved twelve-year old scotch. Simone's dad loved her because, well, she was his child, and he wanted to do better with her than he did with his first born, Tyler, who he'd agreed allow to be adopted by Tyler's mother's next husband. Thus, Tyler's last name was Justice. And her step brother loved her because she was his port in the storm of his perception that both of his fathers hated him (which was miles from the truth) and his own mother cared more about securing the love of Simone's father than nurturing the love of her own son. Everybody in Simone's family tried to love, but there was always something missing. Simone did her best to fill the hole inside of her.

Simone gave away her virginity at age thirteen. By the time she graduated from high school, she'd had eighteen sexual partners. By age twenty, her college career had been stymied by a pregnancy that she wasn't sure wasn't intentional on her part. Simone loved sex. Or at least she thought she did. She wasn't sure. She just kept having it. She was massively in love with the father of her first born. For a while, it felt as if the hole in her soul had been filled by him, and when she became pregnant with his child, it seemed that her life had a chance of becoming complete. But she was wrong.

By the time Simone was struggling with her first opportunity to become complete, Tyler was about to leave Los Angeles. He'd had big fun there. He'd fucked a lot, drank a lot, and solidified that he was his father's son by becoming an alcoholic who could draw the marvel of other drunks with his capacity to drink everyone he faced under the table. Simone had tried alcohol for a short time in college, but found that it only made her feel as if her intestines were turning into jelly. She liked the high, but the aftermath was far too overwhelming.

Tyler, on the other hand, could keep jobs, get ripped, and still not have babies. And that was part of his problem now. By the time he made his way back to Indy, his was smashed by his alcoholism to the point that he didn't even have to avoid bill collectors because he could prove beyond a reasonable doubt that he couldn't pay his bills. He couldn't even secure steady employment. And he was sort of the joke of the family because all ten of his siblings not only had children, but many of them were grandparents. Tyler had prided himself on having no children, now he was the drunk of the family who would probably never have children. He became quite adept at convincing himself that the shit storm he'd developed over his life was what he would have to deal with until the day he died. He was going to die as the drunken uncle.

The Porter family and their propensity for alcohol consumption and their need to appear as functional had been a burden for Simone. She thought she'd overcome that burden when she had a child. But the hole in her soul was far too powerful, and her son's father turned out to be more interested in fucking every woman on the planet than being a family man. Simone was a woman very capably taking care of her son without child support, but struggling emotionally. In her late twenties, she met Morgan Sullivan. He was the best thing ever to happen to her in her life.

Morgan was a highly successful chemical engineer at Mays Chemical. He'd never been married. Even though he'd dated, he'd always been shy around women. He was childless, stable, decent looking, and steeped in the Seventh Day Adventist faith. Simone met him at the annual summer revival in Haughville. The one where she'd taken that glorious car ride home with her brother Tyler when she was only six. Morgan made her feel needed, cherished, wanted, and loved. They married three months after meeting, and they never looked back.

Simone worked at Ely Lily, so they both had great jobs that they loved. Morgan fathered two children with her so they had a terrific family. Simone and Morgan Sullivan had love, family, faith, and more than a few material creature comforts. Life was fantastic. But still, for Simone, there was a void. So, one fine Indy summer day, she finally stopped at the house on 12th Street where her little known brother had once resided. She was overcome to the point of nearly fainting when she learned that he was living there.

Tyler drove home from his menial job at Wal-Mart licking his lips for the pint of rum riding comfortably on the passenger seat of his twenty-year old Ford Bronco SUV. He'd cut down on drinking in the last few years, but only because he couldn't afford to drink as much as he wanted. That was probably for the best, but he had to have something mind-altering to help him to deal with his living and work situations. He'd always been on his own, and so far away. Now he was the drunken uncle who couldn't get a decent job, and had to live in a human zoo. Without his good liquid friend on the passenger seat, he was really quite likely to murder everybody in the crowded house on 12th Street, and take his own life. And then something very strange happened.

After turning onto 12th Street, Tyler could see a strange car that appeared to be parked in front of the house. His fifty-year old eyes couldn't tell for sure until he was about two houses away. He was deciding where to park when he saw a young woman exit the house. She was gorgeous – tall, and built like a brick shit mansion. Her skin was the color of honey mixed with molasses. She almost looked familiar to him. Tyler parked his rust bucket in front of her car. He figured that she was one of his brother's women, even though she looked to be significantly older than his normal type. And then he saw her staring at him from his rear view mirror. He knew right away who she was. He could clearly see the colorful depth of her eyes even from the mirror. Simone, on the other hand, could see much more – feel much more – even from twenty yards away as Tyler leaped out of his vehicle. Simone wanted to run up to her half brother, hug him, and never let him go.

"What're you doing here?" Tyler asked.

"I wanted to see you," Simone answered.

They hugged. "I understand that, Simone, but why now? It's been almost fifteen years."

"It didn't have to be that long, Tyler."

"Touché, baby sister."

They both laughed awkwardly.

"I'm a drunk, Simone. I don't drink nearly as much as I used to, but that's probably because I'm fifty years old and simply can't manage as much drinking as I could when I was thirty. I live here with my parents and a gaggle of my younger sisters and brothers and their children. I have like a hundred of them."

Simone giggled. "You should have grandchildren by now, Tyler."

"Yes I should, but I don't. I hear about it from my family almost every day. How's your life going?"

"Well, we're doing okay. I have three children, and a great husband. We own our own home and we're not having problems with our mortgage."

"You're in Heaven, Simone."

She smiled. "You know what I mean, Tyler."

"I know. But you really are in a way. You look great. You have three children who are obviously very well loved. You have a husband who loves you. You both have great jobs."

"How could you possibly know that?"

"I see it in your eyes, Simone. Besides the fact that you're driving a 2007 Escalade, your eyes scream happiness. So why are you here?"

Simone looked at the ground, and then directly into her brother's eyes. "I don't know. I guess I just want to know you, Tyler. My oldest son wants to know you. I've talked about you to my kids. You're their uncle and they've never seen you other than the picture I showed them."

"What picture?"

"Don't act stupid, Tyler."

"Yeah, that is a great picture of me. I especially love the bow tie."

"I especially love the gleam of hope in your eyes."

And at that moment something extraordinary happened. It was the eyes of Simone Sullivan and Tyler Justice. There was something in the connection of their eyes that made them both very happy, but also made them very uncomfortable.

As she drove away from the house on 12th Street, Simone was completely confused about her feelings. She'd idolized Tyler, even though she'd never really known him. Now she almost felt sorry for him. Like their father, he was a drunk. He was a fifty-year old drunk who was living at home with a gaggle of his much younger siblings – many of whom had never really left home – a seemingly even larger gaggle of their children, and his seventy-five year old mother. He was as far away from the prince she'd always imagined him to be as a Chinese farmer was from being an oil magnate.

Tyler was sitting on the toilet. Evening and night hours were the best time to take a good shit in the crowded house with less possibility of being disturbed, but he went in right after Simone had pulled away even though it was only mid afternoon. He was disturbed by his baby sister's impromptu visit as much as he was pleased by it. He needed to think. The house was about as quiet as Lucas Oil Stadium after a Colts touchdown at that time of the day, but the bathroom offered some refuge. Then, suddenly, there was a knock at the door. It was the un-rhythmic knock of a child.

"Uncle Tyler! Are you in there?" one of his nephews yelled.

"Who the ….," he stopped himself. "What do you want, Allen Iverson Justice? I asked you two minutes ago if any of you had to use the bathroom" Tyler said loudly as he reigned in his anger. Allen was one of two of his nephews who'd been named after an NBA superstar. Tyler thought that the naming was stupid.

There's somebody here to see you!"

"Who?"

"That girl who was here a little while ago!"

Tyler was confused. He wondered why Simone would come back after the awkwardness of only a few minutes earlier. He quickly cleaned himself up. Simone was waiting for him in the living room.

"What's up? Is something wrong?" he asked.

"Do you have gas?" she asked impertinently.

"No. I just had to use the bathroom."

"I mean in your vehicle, Tyler."

"Why? Do you need for me to take you somewhere?"

"No. I need for you to follow me somewhere."

"I've got fuel, Simone. But whether or not I can use it depends on where I'm following you."

"Can you make 16th and Lafayette Rd.?"

"The trip back home might be tricky, but I can certainly make it there," Tyler answered.

Simone held out a five dollar bill to him.

"I can make the round trip. But where are we going?"

"Just follow me," Simone responded. They left quickly without saying another word. She could see the fear and confusion in Tyler's eyes as they pulled into the parking lot. The lot was nearly empty, so it was easy for him to pull up next to her. She exited her vehicle and walked over to his window. He rolled it down. "Why are we here?" he asked.

"It makes me sick to be here, Tyler, but it makes me sicker to not be here," Simone answered.

"I don't understand, Simone."

"I think you do," she said as she opened his vehicle door. She showed him a key.

They were at the Gateway Motel. It was a dump that was used mostly by strippers from the nearby Sunset Strip topless dancing club, and people who smoked crack and couldn't smoke it at home. Tyler followed his baby sister to the door of the room silently. He wanted to speak, but could say nothing. The door to the rickety room had hardly closed before Simone Sullivan and Tyler Justice nearly busted their lips as they slammed their mouths together. They both felt nauseated, but they couldn't stop. It felt just as right as it did wrong.

Simone had purchased three condoms, but they could have used more. They fucked each other as if their souls had been separated at birth, and they were trying to rejoin them. Simone felt sheer heat inside of her as Tyler's penis pounded her all the way to her uterus. She'd screwed quite a few guys, but none of them had her half brother's penile girth in combination with length. All she could see was the photograph of Tyler as a senior in high school as she tried to kill him with her pussy.

Tyler was simply in a world that was spinning. He was as sober as a nun and shocked that he was not only having the best sex of his life without alcohol, but he was having it with his sister.

Over the next few weeks, they screwed once per week. They both exploded onto cloud nine while doing it, felt hugely guilty afterward, pledged to never do it again, and then met at a different motel to do it again.

One evening, as they fucked as if the world was coming to an end, Simone opened her eyes just enough to notice Tyler's face. His eyes were open. He was watching her. Simone responded by pounding at him harder, and looking directly into his eyes. From that point on, they humped with the force of a mule kick, and looked into each other's eyes without fail. It was creepy, but so incredible. They couldn't stop anything they did together sexually.

Simone even took Tyler home to her family. They felt oddly safe. After all, he was her kind of long lost brother. Their weekly meetings were met with encouragement from both families, and the illicit sex they were having made their encounters hard to resist. It was dangerous. It was sinful. They would both burn in hell, if there was such a thing. They didn't care. They were in love. And, most intensely, they were in a lust that they simply were unable to resist.

Tyler got along wonderfully with the Sullivan's. Simone's children accepted him almost immediately as a treasured uncle. Not exposing their forbidden love to their respective families was like resisting eating a dog in Viet Nam. Simone wanted to proclaim to her family that she wanted to marry her half brother, as Tyler wanted to spend the rest of his life with his half sister. He told her often that it was the unrelated halves of them that were so much in love and lust. But such a thing was so unacceptable – especially among African-American families. But then something extraordinary happened.

It was October 3, 2008. Joe Biden had just crushed Sarah Palin in the Vice Presidential debate. Morgan and Tyler were watching the pundits and spinsters further confuse the viewing audience, while Simone was preparing decafinated coffee in the kitchen. All three of them knew that coffee with caffine would have kept them up all night. Simone hesitated at the doorway as she was walking into the living room with the tray. She gazed adoringly at the two men that she loved most in the world. What she was doing was horribly wrong. She was likely going to hell. But she couldn't stop seeing Tyler. He'd taken her sexual places that she could never imagine going. Because of him, she was now having anal sex with Morgan also, and they both loved it. She had a perfect love triangle. No matter what happened between she and Tyler, she was one-hundred percent sure that he would never expose the two of them. No matter what his state in life, he was still a proud man. She sighed as she brought in the coffee.

"Man, I don't care what anybody says. That woman is an idiot," Morgan proclaimed.

"That's true, but she's hot," Tyler answered. "She's got that Tiny Fey thing going, dude."

"Man, you just want to have sex with her eyeglasses."

"I can't help that I love slim glasses on a beautiful woman."

"There's something wrong with you two," Simone commented, forcing a laugh with the skill of Angelina Jolie.

"No, there's something wrong with your brother."

"I've never denied that, Morgan."

All three laughed. They drank their coffees, Tyler quite quickly. He loved being around his found family, and he really liked Morgan. So, he could be around Simone's family for a few hours at a time per month before the guilt of fucking Morgan's wife set in, and he would feel a nausea that his days as a drunk could never touch. He was getting better, time wise, but he still wasn't sure if he ever even wanted to be completely over the guilt.

"I'd best be going," Tyler said. "I've got to be in at seven."

"Wait, Tyler. I'll walk you out," Simone said hurriedly.

"He's a big boy, Simone. I think he knows his way to his car which is parked on the street out front," Morgan grinned.

"I'm going to punish you for that when I get back."

"Okay. Should I wait for you in bed?" Morgan responded, barely able to conceal his joy.

"You'll really be punished even more if you're not," Simone grinned devilishly.

Simone and Tyler exited the house. "That was really cute, Simone," Tyler smiled.

Between the two of you I'm having the most and the best sex that I've had in my entire life," Simone answered seriously.

"What's the matter sis? It's time for us to stop the craziness, isn't it?"

"Yes. But not for the reasons you might think, even though I'm sure that every one of those reasons is excellent."

"Then what is it sis?"

"Stop calling me sis, Tyler," Simone admonished fiercely as they arrived at his car. "I don't know what we are, but I do know that it's evil."

"Okay, Simone."

Simone sighed. "I'm sorry, Tyler. I'm just very confused, and very scared."

"Scared about what?"

"Okay, Tyler. Remember about five weeks ago when we were together back at the Gateway Motel?"

"As strange as this might seem, I remember every single time we've been together."

"That's sweet, Tyler. Do you remember what happened?"

Tyler thought for a second, and then his knees buckled. Simone helped to keep him on his feet. That night five weeks ago had been extraordinary. Tyler couldn't remember his penis ever having gone soft. He and Simone had enjoyed him sexing every orifice sexually available on her body. They started out in the sixty-nine position and finished with her on top of him, banging him so hard that with each bounce, his dick was almost completely outside of her pussy. And then it happened. Their condom of choice was the Magnum, but Tyler had only two of them. He picked up a Trojan condom from the Phillip's 66 gas station in route to the Gateway Motel. Simone felt it first. She was succeeding at actually completely removing Tyler's penis from inside of her, and then slamming it back inside of her without even a near miss when she felt it. As usual, they were gazing into each other's eyes while fucking when they both realized it. The condom had broken. The hesitation was in their eyes only. They couldn't stop fucking. They simply couldn't stop. By the time Simone left the room, neither of them had mentioned the fact that the condom had broken. And in the subsequent five weeks, the incident had completely fallen from their minds.

"What's going on, Simone?"

"I think you know, Tyler."

"What're you going to do?"

"I don't know."

"You can have an abortion."

"You know that's not an option."

"But the baby might be born retarded or something."

"That's possible, but medical statistics don't really support that, Tyler. That guy over in the Netherlands had six children by his own daughter and they turned out to be exceptional despite the blood links, and three of them growing up in absolute captivity."

"Well, the only thing you can do is raise the baby as yours and Morgan's, Simone. I'll do what I can."

"Thanks for the cavalier answer, Tyler. But I know how hard that's going to be on you – having no kids and having your gigantic family tease you about it."

"Well, you just said that it's going to be hard on me."

Simone and Tyler sighed simultaneously, and dropped their gazes to the ground. Tyler kissed his half sister on the cheek, climbed into his car, and took off. Simone trudged back to her house. She wanted to tell Tyler that Morgan had had a vasectomy nearly three years ago, but she couldn't. She figured that she'd tell him soon, but it would turn out to be unnecessary. Morgan was waiting for her, buck naked, when she entered the bedroom. "Is everything okay baby?" he asked.

Simone stripped down naked as quickly as she could, and dove onto her husband. "Tonight, Morgan, I want you to fuck all three of my holes as if you were going to die tomorrow," she said. On that night, he was even better than Tyler.

From the time Tyler Justice left the home of Simone Sullivan until the fatal day, his head spun. He'd made a baby. He was proud of that fact. He'd reveled in his role as the confirmed bachelor. He'd fervently espoused the advantages of having no children, and he'd believed in those advantages. But now, he was going to have a child. He took for granted that Simone's baby was his since she'd gone through the trouble of telling him about the pregnancy the way that she did on the night after the 2008 Vice Presidential debate. He didn't find out about Morgan's vasectomy until two weeks later. Here Tyler was, about to father a child, but he could say nothing about it.

Tyler pulled up in front of his mother's house after a tedious day of work at Wal-Mart. He saw his family members rushing from his mother's house to greet him. There were mothers and children running toward his car. He was more surprised than scared. He should've been more scared. Morgan Sullivan had called. Simone was in trouble.

Simone had decided that abortion was the way to go. She was going to hell for killing her baby. That she was certain of. But she was willing to spend eternity with Satan if it meant that she would spare all of her loved ones – including Tyler and their unborn child – of the pain that she knew they would endure because of the mess that she had caused. She was, and always had been, sick for desiring the boy in the photograph on her grandmother's grand piano in her mind. But what was even sicker was that she didn't regret that she'd had such an incredible physical and emotional relationship with Tyler. She refused to call him her soul mate, but she could never stop the term soul mate from crashing into her mind when it came to Tyler.

Simone Sullivan died because of complications from the pregnancy where the fetus had become detached, and caused her uterus to hemorrhage. The surgeons couldn't stop the bleeding. They didn't know why. It was as if the child wanted to die and take it's mother with it. Morgan was crushed. He wanted to kill the man who'd impregnated his late wife. He wanted Tyler to help him to do so. Tyler calmed Morgan as best he could.   Tyler Justice left Methodist Hospital and walked straight west on Sixteenth Street on a fabulous evening in Indy. The sky was clear, the stars were all but speaking to human ears, and the temperature, for early October, screamed Indian summer. Tyler had killed his sister and the child he would never have been able to claim, but would've loved nonetheless.

All he'd wanted to do was love her. He climbed onto the freshly remodeled bridge at West 16th Street just east of Milburn Street, and dove into Fall Creek in about two feet of water. His blood drew fish that probably would only have been known to exist in the creek by marine academics. He'd killed all that had come to matter to him. It seemed only right that his death fueled lives that maybe five percent of the human population even knew existed. Nobody could've convinced Tyler Justice that he didn't deserve to die.

Between Holidays

A Short Story

By

E. Marvin Neville

Cornell Dean had had enough. He'd come to the family home of Alisa Crowe on Grandview Drive in north Indy for a July fourth barbeque. What he got was the Hatfield's and the McCoy's. It was the third date for Cornell and Alisa, and he was willing to do something that he hated in order to at least get to third base, and, hopefully bed her that night. That thing was to attend a family function that was filled with nothing but strangers to him. He was an only child born to only children. He had no discernable family, so everywhere he went he was pretty much a stranger.

Cornell was a computer engineer in a small company with three partners and a handful of employees that specialized in streamlining the effectiveness of the computer systems of companies large and small. Their customers were offered two ways to pay the fee – a large flat fee, or a small percentage of the savings over a set number of years. Trident Consulting preferred the latter, and, most of the time, that was what they got. Trident Consulting was quite successful. Alisa's employer wanted Trident's services in a bad way, and they sent Alisa to open the dialogue. They'd seen one another numerous times before. They'd never spoken until that day. Cornell had never been a ladies man, and

Alisa had always attached herself to bad boys. Cornell was now highly financially successful, and Alisa was ready to at least try a different type of man. It was an issue of timing, and they both thought that they'd hit the jackpot. After only two dates, Alisa had impressed him with her knowledge of computers along with her prolific beauty, and the fact that she was a single mother of a well schooled teenaged son who was excelling at Crispus Attucks Medical Magnet High School. Alisa truly liked the fact that Cornell was a very successful and highly educated businessman who'd never had so much as a speeding ticket, had no children, and was really one of the best looking dark-skinned Black men she'd ever known. She'd always preferred light-skinned Black men. Cornell had turned her head with his intelligence. He'd made vibrant love to her mind. She wanted her family to meet him. She had no idea that a battle between the Crowe's and the Johnson's would ensue.

It all started with one of Alisa's nephews, already drunk, pulling up to park along Grandview among at least a dozen other vehicles. Apparently, he nearly ran over the Johnson family matriarch as she checked the mailbox on the edge of the road. One argument from the Crowe family was that it was July fourth. There was no mail delivery. But both families knew that Greta Johnson was as mentally infirm as a drinking glass on a tree branch. The Crowe's put the argument forth anyway. The Crowe's back yard was littered with verbal combatants, mostly adults. Alisa and Cornell watched from the basement window. It was a familiar place for Alisa. She never liked the battles. She avoided them whenever she could. "I'm sorry about this," she sighed to Cornell. "It happens at least once a year for some stupid reason or other. But we always make up and look out for each other."

"Don't worry about it, Cornell answered. "But I think I should leave."

"Why?"

"Well, I've never seen anything like this before."

"Yeah, but you're an only child."

"I'm not going to apologize for that, Alisa."

"I'm sorry. I don't mean it like that. I'm just saying that when you get two big families living next to each other for forty years, things like this sometimes happen."

"I'm sure they do, but that doesn't make me feel any more comfortable."

Alisa looked sad. "Does this mean we're off for tonight?" she asked.

"You call me when you're on your way, and I'll give you directions to my condo. But don't wait too late. The closer it gets to fireworks time, the more heavy the traffic downtown," he smiled.

Alisa smiled. Her teeth were so perfect, and her dark brown eyes so piercing from her light brown skin. She was gorgeous. "I'll call you the second this shit settles down," she said. She kissed him on the lips. It was their first kiss. But Cornell was anticipating much more that night.

Cornell's plan had been to spend the afternoon with the Crowe's, and leave with Alisa by no later than eight pm. The annual July fourth fireworks from the top of the Chase Bank building – the tallest in downtown Indianapolis – were scheduled to start at nine forty seven pm. He had fine wine, cheeses, shrimp cocktail and even various salads ready for a romantic fireworks viewing from the terrace of his tenth floor condo at Villaggio At Page Pointe, at Fletcher Pointe on the south side of downtown Indy where South Street, East Street, and Virginia Avenue merged. The view of downtown was spectacular, and it was almost as if one could see the crew shooting off the fireworks from the vantage point of his balcony without the benefit of binoculars. Cornell figured that if he didn't get laid that night, he was at least going to taste the inside of Alisa's mouth. But other sinister forces were at work.

Cornell exited through the front door, away from the action. The action found him.

"Where you goin', motherfucker?" an unseen voice shouted.

Cornell ignored it. After all, he didn't know a single soul except for Alisa, and she was inside the house, and the voice was overwhelmingly male. But then he heard footsteps from behind. Instinctively he turned around. There was a well muscled, well tattooed light skinned man stomping toward him. It was Brent Johnson. He was, by far, the most criminal of the Johnson clan, which, through their copious history, had enough petty criminals to blow apart a Thanksgiving cornucopia. They just seemed to tumble out of their respective mothers like apples from a busted bag. The Crowe's weren't criminally driven, but they were of the thinking that petty crime wasn't so bad, and even helpful. Their good relationship with the Johnson's kept the Johnson's out of the Crowe's house. But there was the more than the occasional dust up, and Cornell found himself right in the middle of one.

Fighting was something that Cornell had lost at mostly up through middle school, and had been able to educate himself out of through high school. Educate meant that he would convince his adversary that fighting was the wrong thing to do, and sometimes the adversary would even feel ashamed. But Cornell was sure that the education method would fall on deaf ears in the case facing him now. Brent was charging for no other reason than he was drunk and ready to escalate. That was where Brent made his mistake. "Who the fuck are you?" Brent yelled.

"Look, man. I was here to visit Alisa, but now I'm leaving," Cornell responded calmly, even though his gut was churning with fear.

"Why? Were you the one who almost ran over my momma?"

"I thought you guys had already determined who that was," Cornell answered.   Cornell started to back away in hope of turning around and walking away, but Brent had something else in mind. Cornell sensed it, and planted himself in preparation. It was clear from the better muscle definition that Brent was right handed. It was easy for Cornell to duck the wild right-handed swing from Brent, plant a solid right fist into his solar plexus, and slam a left cross on Brent's Jaw as he doubled over from the stomach shot. Cornell was sure that his own left wrist was broken (it turned out that he was mistaken) as he watched Brent Johnson collapse to the ground. Cornell looked up as he shook his left wrist in an effort to dismiss the pain, and saw a coal black man, Brent's older brother Glen, throw a three foot wooden fence picket at him as he charged Cornell.

Cornell wondered where a person got such a thing. He dug in for another physical confrontation, but the police finally arrived. Cornell decided that he was going to press charges.

Alisa arrived at Cornell's condo well after the fireworks had ended. They spent time on his balcony. They nibbled at some of the food, and scarcely sipped at the wine. An evening that, for Cornell, was supposed to start a serious relationship at most and semi-regular sex at least had devolved into awkwardness and somber.

"I'm sorry about today," Alisa said, as they sat on his balcony, unable to look into each others eyes as they had before the incident.

"Why are you sorry? You had nothing to do with it," he responded.

"I know, but I invited you."

"Did you invite me to a fight?"

"No."

"So what's the problem?" Cornell asked.

"You pressed charges, Cornell."

"And that's a problem because?"

Alisa sighed. "It's not that serious, Cornell."

"It was to me. I thought I'd broken my wrist. And he doesn't even know me."

"I know, I know. He didn't mean any harm. It's something we all go through."

"No. It's not, Alisa. The man committed a serious crime," Cornell said.

"He didn't mean to hurt you."

"So why did he attack me?"

"He was drunk."

"So I shouldn't prosecute him because he was drunk?"

"You don't understand."

"No. I understand clearly. Are you fucking him?"

"No," Alisa answered.

"But you've fucked him before, right?"

Alisa shook her head as if trying to clear her mind. "He's the father of my child," she exclaimed. "But that has nothing to do with it."

"It has everything to do with it," Cornell said as he rose from his seat, and walked to his front door, opening it. "I'll walk you to your car."

Alisa tried to convince Cornell that he was doing the wrong thing in prosecuting Brent Johnson. She not only tried to make him understand that Brent was a good guy she told him that nobody from either family would corroborate Cornell's story. They'd known each other for forty years. Cornell espoused to Alisa that he was a serious businessman in America, and that his word was solid. Alisa begged Cornell. Brent might end up spending many years in prison. He didn't deserve that. "I disagree. That's exactly what a criminal deserves," Cornell said. Their relationship essentially ended as he closed the door to her car. Or at least he thought it had ended.

On Monday July seventh, Cornell walked out of the Landmark Center – a high rise office building at Eleventh and Meridian Streets on the northern edge of downtown Indy – as he'd done for years, primed, dressed, and ready for his walk home. It was about a six mile walk there and back, but it was one of his ways of staying in shape as he worked more than he probably should have, and definitely exercised less as he tail spun through his thirties toward his forties. He kept clothing in his office so that he was always clean for business, yet prepared for his daily walks. As he stepped onto Pennsylvania Street, he noticed a woman standing on the east side of the street. She was tall, dark, and he could see the sun from the west glistening off the perspiration on her ample breasts. He knew a beautiful Black woman when he saw one. He was about to cross the street near the newly and expensively refurbished Marion County Library at St. Claire St. when he noticed, upon checking the one-way south bound traffic, that the tall, dark woman was only a few dozen yards behind him. He thought little of it until he saw her still – maintaining the same distance – as he approached South St. His instinct kicked in. It was like the guy on Oprah Winfrey who clamed that most people who are about to become victims of crimes get an inner feeling that they almost always ignored. Cornell decided to not ignore his.

Cornell kept south on Pennsylvania until he arrived at South St. where he turned west. The brand new, gorgeous, and fabulously imposing Lucas Oil Stadium loomed only a block away. He walked quickly past The Slippery Noodle blues bar, and turned back north onto Illinois St. at the Whistle Stop tavern across from Union Station, and the Post Office. The woman lost sight of him, and hustled up to

Illinois St. She went inside of the Whistle Stop. She didn't see him. She checked the men's room quickly, and even the ladies room. He was nowhere to be found. She tried to go into the kitchen, but was stopped by the bartender. "May I help you?" the blonde White bartender asked.

"I'm looking for a guy – a dark skinned Black man. Bald, wearing a cream colored shirt with a black and red tie with black pants."

"I haven't seen anybody like that."

The Black woman sneered. "He had to come in here," she said.

"I don't know what he had to do, Miss. All I know is that I haven't seen him."

The Black woman sighed, and then made a quick move for the kitchen. But the bartender had anticipated the move, and blocked her. It was apparent that she could handle herself physically. But so could the Black woman. The problem was that the Black woman would be the one to go to jail if she caused a commotion. She relented. She walked back outside. Cornell was waiting for her. He glared at her with disdain. "Is there something I can do for you?" he asked.

"Excuse me?" she responded.

"Don't insult me by acting like you haven't been following me since I left work. Who are you?"

"I don't know what you're talking about."

"Mary, the bartender, is calling the police as we speak. They like me here at the Whistle Stop. They don't want to lose my business," Cornell smiled slyly.

The woman sighed deeply. "Karla Johnson," she whispered.

"Karla Johnson? You must be Brent Johnson's sister."

"I'm his wife."

"Terrible thing, but I got the spiel from Alisa already. His assault on me ruined what was going to be a great date, I might add. But I'm pursuing charges against your husband, and nothing you say is going to change that."

"Can I at least get a few minutes of your time – even if my effort is futile."

Cornell liked the fact that Karla had said futile. "Did Alisa tell you where I worked?"

"She and Brent used to be high school sweethearts. The two families are weird, but there really is a lot of love there," Karla offered.

"I see. So they reserve their hatred for complete strangers?"

"It's not like that, Mr. Dean. Can you call off the pit bull in there so we can have a beer and talk for a few minutes? I'll buy."

Karla was beautiful, and classy. She'd called him Mr. Dean, and offered to buy drinks. Cornell accepted. Karla Johnson launched into a well-meaning campaign about how Brent had been born into a petty criminal family that had spanned at least four generations, but that they'd never committed any serious crimes, such as murder, that she'd ever known of. In fact, there was more love among the Johnson's than she'd experienced with any alleged law biding families she'd ever known.

"So your husband attacking me was an expression of that love?" Cornell asked skeptically.

"Everybody was drunk," Karla answered.

"I had a decent buzz myself, and I didn't want to assault anybody."

"But you handled yourself quite well."

Cornell smiled. "Yes, I did. But I was lucky. Your husband assumed that he could kick my ass, and, nine times out of ten, he would probably be right. He underestimated me, Karla. But that's really irrelevant. He broke the law."

"Haven't you ever broken the law, Mr. Dean?"

"Yes. But never while trying to break another person's jaw, or trying to separate them from their money, or anything against another person. I have, however, driven under the influence, accidentally opened somebody else's mail, and I have received a number of speeding tickets. I have a lead foot."

Karla giggled. "I assume you've never been to jail."

"Not even to bail somebody out, Karla."

"Not everybody in jail is bad, Mr. Dean."

"Please, call me Cornell. And most of them have not only broken the law, they've gotten caught."

"So, you're going ahead with this, Cornell?"

"I'd rather die than not snitch against somebody like your husband."

"We have children, Cornell."

"And you consciously produced them with a convicted felon."

Karla seemed conflicted, but still spoke on Brent's behalf. "I hope you live for me to see you again, Cornell Dean."

"I hope that wasn't a threat from the wife of a really good guy," he responded.

Karla got up and left the Whistle Stop as if she struggled against storming out angrily. Cornell decided that the next day was a good time to start carrying the pistol he was licensed to carry.

It was early August, and Central Indiana had been given a reprieve from the blistering heat and hydration sapping humidity that had plagued June and July like an equatorial thermal blanket. Cornell liked that because temperatures hovering around eighty degrees made his walks home from work more palatable. He was the last to leave the office as usual, and was startled to see a smiling Alisa waiting for him in the corridor outside of the locked doors. She looked like a slightly older version of actor Eva Mendez, with a beautifully shaped head like that of female basketball star and ESPN analyst, Kara Lawson. Cornell, however, wasn't stupid. He switched his briefcase to his left hand, reached beneath the gathers of his jogging suit trousers, and released the safety switch on his thirty-eight snub nose as if he were scratching an errant itch. He took a view of the corridor from the all glass door as he unlocked it.

"It's not like that, Cornell," Alisa smiled.

"Not like what?"

"I know where you live, man. If I was going to set you up, I wouldn't risk my job."

"It's good to know that you'd rather keep your job than save a human life," Cornell said as he wearily locked the office door.

"That's not fair, Cornell."

"I know. You've got an eighteen year old daughter to feed."

"Look, man. I came here to apologize to you. But I don't need this shit."

"You're right. I'm sorry, Alisa. It's just that I've never had somebody that I really liked defend somebody who tried to kick my ass."

"You said liked. Does that mean you don't like me anymore?"

Cornell sighed and looked at his feet. "I don't know, Alisa."

"Look, you were right. Brent had no reason to attack you, and he did. I've never seen him like that."

Cornell decided to keep the fact that he'd spent time with Brent's wife Karla to himself.

"Anyway, I thought that two of our three dates were great. I was wondering if you were willing to try for three out of four," Alisa lamented.

"Can I call you in a few days?"

"Of course, Cornell, and I really hope you do. You pick the time. You pick the place. I guarantee you that it'll be worth it, Cornell," Alisa said with a sincerity that made him want to rush her into his office and make sure that three out of the four dates were great. Alisa smiled with the shyness of a catholic virgin as she walked away.

Cornell wanted to call her the next day, but he waited three days. He'd set up his condo like the love nest it was supposed to be on that past July fourth , and was eagerly anticipating calling her once he got home. He made sure that his gun was always close, just in case, but he had a really good feeling about the night to come. And then something very strange happened.

Cornell was leaving his office as usual when he saw a familiar, yet quite startling sight. Back at her initial perch on the east side of Pennsylvania St. was Karla Johnson. Now he was sure that something was going on. She smiled when she saw him, waved, and ran across the fairly busy street to join him. Once again, Cornell released the safety on his gun in the holster beneath his jogging pants. "What are you doing here?" he asked as she jogged to a breathless stop.

"I wanted to see you."

"Why?" he asked

"I believe you."

"You believe me?"

"Listen. All I've known is guys like Brent. I've met guys like you, but I always thought of them as, well, pussies."

"I see," Cornell responded. "So guys who get good grades, graduate from college with honors, and start successful businesses out of college are pussies?"

"Well, yes. But that's only because I didn't know any better.

"So you wanted to see me to tell me I'm a pussy?"

"No. I wanted to see you to tell you that you're the most fascinating man I've ever met. I wanted to tell you that you're right about me bringing children into the world by a criminal, and that the fact that I did says a lot about my own self esteem and self worth."

"I don't remember saying all that, Karla."

"It was easy to read between the lines, Cornell."

"So you don't care that I'm going to put your husband in prison?"

"I care. I don't want him to go to prison. But he put himself there, not me, and not you."

"Well, I'm sorry that it came to this."

"In a way, I'm not. I might be losing the man I love. But do I really love him? I mean, have I just accepted what I thought was the only thing there for me?"

"I've got to be honest, Karla. That question is too deep for me to answer."

"I'm not asking you to answer it, Cornell. But I do have something to ask of you."

"I'm scared. This is starting to kind of feel like a setup."

"I understand that, but I'm going to ask anyway. I want to get to know you, Cornell. Just as a friend if that's all you want. You've already committed serious foreplay on my mind. If all you ever do is make love to it for however long I know you, I'll be very lucky," Karla said.

Cornell was stunned. "You're a lot smarter than I gave you credit for," he said.

"Maybe I am. Maybe I'm not. I just want you to know that you can trust me because I want you to get to know me. Maybe somebody like you can get to like somebody like me."

"I don't help unhappy women cheat."

"I know. I just want to know if you can help an unhappy woman be happy."

"Is there some way I can reach you without bringing the terrorists down on me?"

Karla reached into her cleavage, pulled out a small piece of paper, and handed it to Carnell. She walked away without saying a word, and Cornell was unable to speak. He saw Alisa that night, but he was just strong enough to keep the intruding thoughts of Karla from interfering with the evening. In fact, Alisa threw herself at him as if she were a fifty year old virgin. Cornell caught every pitch like a Hall of Fame baseball catcher. By the time the lovemaking was done the sheets on the bed were as wet as an overused sponge.

He called Karla the next day. He really wanted to test to see if she knew anything about him and Alisa. If she did, she played it like a professional spy. She seemed only to want to talk to him. They spoke at length that night. Well, he spoke. She mostly listened and asked questions. Karla really seemed to want to change her life.

As Labor Day, and Brent Johnson's trial date approached, it was all good for Cornell Dean. But he was still cautious. His relationship with Alisa Crowe was growing stronger by the day, as was his friendship with Karla Johnson. It was clear that he and Karla wanted each other badly. They crossed the line on Labor Day.

Alisa had asked Cornell to her family's house on Grandview for Labor Day even though she knew that he would decline because of the assault by her former love Brent Johnson on July fourth. She was right about the decline, but she was wrong about the reason why. Cornell had finally given his address to Karla. He could no longer resist her willingness to grow mentally and emotionally. She'd made love to his mind by trying to become a better person, and wanting for him to be part of that growth.

Cornell walked down to the entrance of the complex to let Karla in to make sure that she hadn't been followed. She hadn't. The doors to the elevator had barely closed before they pounced upon one another. Their physical fit was near perfect. She was nearly his height. Her tongue tasted like Belgian mint, and her lips were covered with raspberry lip gloss that was just thin enough to allow for firry kissing without jaw breaking slippage. Had the building been a Manhattan New York level skyscraper complex, Cornell and Karla would've been naked when the elevator door opened. They kissed hard all the way to Cornell's condo, and never made it past the tile in front of his door on the inside. The loving was worth it. By the end, her backside and his knees were heavily bruised. Neither of them had had such a lover where the connection was so deep that the minds had relinquished all thought. It was white hot fucking. And it was only the first time between them. If Cornell had had second thoughts about putting Brent Johnson away in prison, that notion was now eliminated.

Karla scrambled to her feet once they were done. "I've got to go," she said.

"Where'd you tell him you were going?" Cornell asked.

"I didn't. He left, and I called you."

"So he has no idea where you are. Why hurry?"

"This was wrong, Cornell."

"Yes it was, but it was so right."

Karla ventured a small smile, gathered up her clothes in one fell swoop, and dressed as if her clothes were joined as one. Cornell wasn't as adept. He'd just gotten his underwear on as she slammed the door behind her. Once dressed, he chased after her. There was no sign of her in the building. He went outside and ran up Virginia Ave. He'd never seen her car. When he turned to make his way back to his condo, he was shocked by the sight before him. There they were. Brent, Glen, Alisa Crowe, and Karla Johnson were between him and the entrance of his condo. He'd been scammed by something fierce by the best pussy he'd ever had. His first instinct was to scream for help, but he knew that by the time other area residents recognized anything, it would be too late. He decided to make a break first, get past the blockade, and scream then. Glen pulled out a gun. "Keep your mouth shut. You're coming with us," he said.

Cornell shook his head. "If you're going to kill me, you're going to do it right here and now. I'm not coming anywhere with you motherfuckers," he exclaimed.

"I'm sorry, Cornell. But I can't let you put them in prison," Alisa said as she ran for her car.

Karla said nothing. She merely looked terrified.

Brent pulled a gun also. He and his brother Glen strode purposefully toward Cornell. Cornell prepared himself for some sort of a fight. He knew that he wasn't going to win, but he was determined that he wasn't going anywhere with them. He was going to die right there, right now. Two shots rang out.

It was a sweltering day in Indy, and the numerous trees at Crown Hill Cemetery did almost nothing to allay the heat. Karla Johnson stood nearly one hundred yards away from the burial scene, tears streaming down her face. She was startled by someone behind her. The minister at the burial pleaded with God to accept the souls of Brent and Glen Johnson. Karla turned to see Cornell behind her. "Why'd you do it?" he asked.

Karla wiped the tears from her face with a handkerchief. "Because they were going to kill you," she answered.

"No. I mean why'd you set me up in the first place?"

"I didn't set you up, Cornell. I set them up. I set them all up, including Alisa. I might go to prison. But I couldn't let them kill you. I had to stop the cycle, Cornell. Alisa's telling the truth. She's going to testify against me for shooting them – for setting them up."

"She's going to lose, Karla. You're going to win. And whether you really want me or not, I'll be here for you every step of the way. You put your life on the line for me. I've already got the best defense attorneys in the state to represent you."

"I don't know how long it'll take me to finally understand that I did the right thing by killing my husband and his brother, but I'll be running to the man who made me realize who I am when it's all over," she said. They kissed passionately, hoping for a new beginning for them together.

HATED STRANGERS

A Short Story

By

E. Marvin Neville

Ben Gentry was fed up. He blamed mostly himself for where he was in life, but there was ample room to blame some outside influences. Ben was a college educated Black man who'd squandered his life by falling in love. He'd fallen in love with a woman named cocaine. He'd do her any way he could ingest her. He'd snort her, smoke her, he'd even mainlined her by way of hypodermic needle in between his toes. He'd often wondered how it would feel to have a cocaine enema.

By the time Ben quit the best paying job he'd ever held under the guise of managerial and philosophical differences he was thirty-thousand dollars in debt. He was a very smart man, but his need to be high every day severely affected his judgment. Sure, the IUPUI Parking and Transportation Operations Supervisor position paid him well for a public sector position. And the benefits were admirable. But he knew within months after resigning from the job in January of 2004 that he should've stuck it out despite the fact that the department treated it's hourly, non-benefited life blood workers as if they were snails beneath salt coated boot soles. He regretted now more than ever, in 2008, that he had let the thirteen dollars and ninety five cents per hour go. He was thirty thousand dollars in debt now, and President George W. Bush was making sure that he, a college educated man, couldn't get a job sweeping floors at a floor sweeping factory. But it wasn't just George W. Bush that had held him back. His former bosses at IUPUI, the director and the assistant director, told potential employers that, even though they couldn't prove it, he'd stolen money from the department. In a tight economy, that alone was enough to keep potential employers from taking a very small chance on him. He'd never stolen money from the department. He'd merely borrowed it and returned it.

Ben had entered a recovery program in February of 2004, and it had helped him. For four years he'd been clean with about one-hundred and fifty three relapses. But by March of 2008, he was completely clean. After four years of touch and go, he'd finally had completely lost the desire to use cocaine. He should've been exploding in ecstasy. Instead, the months of complete sobriety had turned out to be much worse than the years of attempted recovery.

In April 2008, both of his elderly parents had died. They left him the house. But even though he hadn't held the cocaine parties that he might have only days before, he wished that he had. He just as well could've just partied until the state of Indiana kicked him onto the street. But he kept trying to stop the shit storm he'd created from completely consuming him. He failed. And it was one final rejection in early August of 2008 that celebrated that failure.

It had been a tough four years and nearly ten months for Ben – fighting his addiction. But what had been really hard was the fact that he couldn't seem to find decent work. His job in a doctor's office had garnered him severe migraine headaches. It seemed that doctors cared little about the well being of their employees in the work environment, and merely wanted done what they said when they said it. For nearly a year and a half, Ben worked for an inventory company. He liked the work very much, but the number of hours available every two weeks was so spastically erratic that it was impossible to know how much his bi-weekly pay would be, and even then, it wasn't much. Besides, the atmosphere there was so Black ghetto that he frequently found himself using the word motherfucker as a noun, adjective, and adverb in a single seven word sentence. Ben loved his job scoring standardized tests for primary education students. He could experience the thoughts of ten year olds, and set up his own system of not only exceeding production levels, but exceeding accuracy standards. But, alas, it was project work. If there were no projects, there was no work. He spent June and July of 2008 completely without employ, and the Bush economy made it difficult for even a Nobel Laureate to get a job. By the time he got a job at the Value City Department Store at Pike Plaza on the final day of July 2008, he didn't really care much about working. He was ready to die. Ben's depression was such that he'd been able to secure a prescription for thirty Zoloft tablets, and he had a cache of drugs left behind by his late parents. Using a fifth of rum as his wash down agent, he decided to alternate between ingesting the Zoloft and some Hydrocodone pills left behind by his father. The heart, blood pressure, and cholesterol medications he left behind might have caused him some pain, according to research he'd done on the internet. He wanted to slip away quietly and painlessly. He'd had enough pain in his miserable life. He picked rum only because it had been his drink of choice for as long as he could remember. The rum tasted better than ever as he swigged it to down the pills. He hoped only that he'd be able to finish the bottle before he slipped into the darkness of death. There was no sense in wasting good rum.

Ben started to dream. He felt wetness on his body. He looked down to see that he was covered in blood. At that point, he realized that he wasn't dreaming. He wasn't dead. And it took him about ten minutes to realize that the blood wasn't his own. He would've panicked had he not been too drunk still to maintain consciousness. He panicked later.

Relaine Gordon was slogging through the knee level tar thick mess that she'd made into her life. Her fake life had been good. She had deftly defrauded Social Security, welfare, and numerous other family assistance agencies for dozens of years, but she got tripped up when her six-year old middle son took an ounce of marijuana from her live-in boyfriend's stash to school for show and tell. Relaine ended up in prison for six months, and her three children were sent to Gary, IN to live with her mother. She'd been released in 2006, got her children back in 2007, and ordered to pay restitution to the agencies she'd defrauded. One good thing was that her boyfriend was a three-time looser for major amounts of drugs – the authorities seized eleven pounds from their house after the show and tell incident – and was now about two years into a mandatory twenty year stint in federal prison. What was good about that was that he had nearly one-hundred thousand dollars stashed away, and only two people knew about it. She was forbidden to make contact with him. She figured that she'd worry about him in twenty years. She couldn't let on that she had the money, so she worked at Value City at Pike Plaza, making meager wages, and paid her restitution monthly from the proceeds of her union with her former boyfriend. She was committed to changing her life. She had to be a better person for the sake of her children.

Ben was petrified all day. He'd only been employed at Value City for a few weeks, and he was praying that nobody noticed that he was freaking out inside. Nobody seemed to notice. His six hour shift was made only slightly tolerable by one person, Relaine Gordon. She'd been very sweet to him from the moment they'd first met. She'd been, and continued to be, mildly flirtatious with him. She wasn't his type physically. She was dark and more than fairly overweight. But she was smart, and she didn't use profanity nearly as much as her Midwestern female peers. She was from Gary, Indiana, which might have been another deterrent from attraction accept for the fact that she seemed to be able to make him feel comfortable. He figured that he might've even spent time with her had he not met her too late. He was ready to die, and she wasn't powerful enough in his life to stop him. That made him even sadder.

That night, Ben made sure that he was going to die. He doubled the dosage of pills. But once again he awoke the following morning covered in blood that didn't belong to him.

Relaine watched Ben walk into the store. He appeared even more sullen than usual – if that was possible. But he was cute in a brooding kind of way. She figured he couldn't be much worse of a choice than the drug dealing Neanderthals who'd fathered her children. He was light skinned – which she liked – and smart. So were a lot of other guys she knew, though. But there was something dark and mysterious about Ben Gentry. She decided to approach him. The store wasn't open yet, so she met him at the time clock in the break room. Ben was alone when she arrived.

"What's up Ben?" Relaine asked.

"Same old shit, different day," he replied.

"Are you okay?"

"I make seven dollars an hour. What do you think?"

"Excuse me for caring."

Ben shook two nights of unseen terror out of his head. "I'm sorry, Relaine," he said. "It's been a tough couple of nights. I haven't been able to sleep."

"Why?"

"I don't know. It happens to me sometimes."

"Have you seen a doctor?"

"I make seven dollars an hour, Relaine."

"I don't have any problem seeing a doctor, Ben."

"You're a single mother with three minor children."

"I don't see how that matters."

"You're right. Was there something you wanted?"

"Well, I was going to ask you if you wanted to have a beer after work. But I think I change my mind."

Ben thought about the events of the last two nights. Perhaps a change of pace would be helpful for him – would remove him from the sheer terror he'd experienced. "Don't change your mind. I'll even buy the first round," he said.

"But you only make seven dollars an hour."

"That's why I said I'd buy the first round. Beer's expensive."

They both laughed. They had no clue about what was going to happen that afternoon after work.

Ben and Relaine walked to the nearby Claude and Annie's. She actually brought him out of his funk as they talked and drank. He even bought the third round. And then the Channel Twelve news came on. Two women had been murdered horrifically according to Andrea Morehead, the female Black anchor for WTHR News. Ben Gentry had known them both.

Murdered on successive nights were both the Director and Assistant Director at IUPUI Parking and Transportation Services (the two lesbian bitches that had bad mouthed him to numerous potential employers). They'd each been brutally sexually assaulted and stabbed to death. Ben couldn't swallow. He became nauseous. It was the first time in his life that he was happy about his body preparing to vomit. He excused himself and ran to the bathroom, where he was barely able to contain the explosion before he made it to the commode. By the time his dry heaves ended, he was certain that he could see small portions of his intestines floating amongst the thick, putrid muck from his stomach. He washed his face with cold water, and made his way back to Relaine. She looked concerned.

"Are you alright, Ben?" she asked.

"I haven't been feeling well all day, Relaine. I just blew chunks the size of asteroids into the toilet, and I think I'd better leave before the staff here finds out."

"Will you be at work tomorrow?"

"I'll do my best. I need to make this up to you."

Relaine smiled. She thought it very sweet that a sick man was more worried about her than himself.

Ben was almost too shaky to drive, but he rushed home as quickly as he could. He knew what he had to do, and he went right to work. He set up his video camera in his bedroom, turned it on to record, and loaded up on the same amount of booze and pills he'd ingested the night before. The next thing he knew, he was waking up the next morning. And what he saw astounded him so much that not only was his mouth agape like a sick Catholic priest finding out that the boy he'd been having sex with was a transsexual, but the slobber from his mouth was literally cascading like a waterfall.

Relaine sighed as she entered her tiny house on Indy's near west side. It was a neighborhood removed from tough Haughville by about a half mile, but much closer to it culturally. It didn't bother her much, though. She was, after all, from Gary. What did bother her, however, was the life situation she'd put herself in. Had she not committed the frauds, she might've been able to secure better employment, which would've meant that she wouldn't be bellowed over by her overbearing manager – a tiny half Japanese half Black fireplug with a voice the size of a foghorn, and an inferiority complex that was even bigger. She lorded over Relaine more than she did any other employee. At least that was what Relaine thought. Relaine wanted to knock the holy shit out of her. In fact, she was sure that she would've taken great pleasure in beating the manager within an inch of her life, reviving her daily, and beating her more until her face was a swollen mass of blood-red bruises. And then, Relaine would cut off her eyelids, and gleefully watch the life drain out of her manager's eyes as she beat her to death. She smiled. "I should be a writer," she thought.

Just then, her youngest son cried out for her. Apparently, the older two boys were teasing him. She loved her boys. They were basically good boys. But sometimes, she truly hated their guts. Their lives consisted mostly of bitching, whining, and deceit, and more bitching whining and deceit. Her older two boys had experienced a short life of privilege by way of ill-gotten gains, and now, even though their lives were still decent, they were experiencing the negative consequences of that good life. Now, to Relaine, they were more like little girls – except smellier. Because she was a staunch proponent of corporal but non-abusive punishment for children by their parents, she could never beat them like she wanted to beat her manager. She decided that it would be better to choke them to death. Then, she'd watch the light of life extinguish in their eyes without all the blood of a beating. And she could let them savor just how ungrateful they'd been as they died. She had other scenarios in mind for her creepy probation officer, and her son's fathers. She smiled again. "I really think I could write a book," she thought again. "What the hell are you guys doing in there?" she screamed as she made her way to her son's room. She knew she could never live without them, her creepy probation officer, or even her maniac manager and her imprisoned former lovers. She'd been weak before her own incarceration. She felt like she was strong now, and only getting stronger. Maybe she would write that book.

Ben couldn't breathe now. He called off sick at Value City even though he'd really wanted to see Relaine that day. He watched himself wake up the night before on the video tape, and he absolutely didn't recognize the man he was watching who was wearing his face. That man hated White women like Hitler hated himself. Ben wasn't like that. He'd even dated several White women. But Ben couldn't remove his own eyes from the eyes of his alter ego. It was as if they were communicating in person. And Ben couldn't help but to listen. His alter ego pontificated at length about how affluent Whites were taking downtown Indy back, and the women were moving about alone after twilight as if they owned the world, as if nothing could hurt them. Yet he could take a walk to Lee's Liquor Store at five pm, at clear daylight, and see White women exiting office buildings holding the longest key on their key rings between the ring and middle fingers of their strong hand as he walked by them. Even during the height of rush hour foot and vehicle traffic on the corner of 10th and Illinois they would do that when they saw him. It was humiliating. They would look at the ground as Ben passed them by. Ben understood. A female alone needed to protect herself. But his alter ego didn't understand. Through Ben, he'd once seen a White woman leaving the Stutz Building at 11th and Senate go through extraordinary lengths to avoid him on the street, and then turn around and hold a conversation with a White man who looked as if he'd burrowed through a dumpster for his own skin. Ben had been as clean shaven and well dressed as a Black lawyer who was simply out for afternoon exercise. Ben now clearly understood what his alter ego was saying to him. It had taken two attempts at his life to see it.

Ben returned to work the day after his call off. Relaine was genuinely concerned. He'd been at work for an hour on the receiving dock when she approached him without caring who saw her, or what they thought. "You feeling better, Ben?" she asked.

"I feel better than I have in a very long time," he answered happily.

Relaine had never seen him so happy. "What kind of drugs are you on?" she asked sarcastically.

"I'm on life, baby. And I believe I promised to make up for the other night."

"You did."

"Look, according to our schedules, we're both off this Saturday. I guarantee you that I can cook up a meal at your house that'll please you and your sons as long as they like fish."

Relaine smiled thoughtfully. According to the terms of her parole, she really wasn't supposed to forge involvements with men. But it was already too late for that. "They like perch," she said.

"Perch is one of my many specialties," Ben answered as sexily as he possibly could.

The day turned out to be a smash. The perch was so good that Relaine had to buy more to satisfy her ravenous sons. Ben was good with her boys, too. He was fatherly, yet respectful that he wasn't their father. Relaine wanted to fuck him right on the kitchen table with her sons watching.

Over the next few weeks, Ben went on a mini killing spree. He wanted to kill the John McCain supporter who called Barack Obama an Arab. He wanted to ram a double sided knife into her vagina, first vertically, and then horizontally, creating a bloody cross. But she was too far away. So he chose his targets close by, and carefully. It was so much easier than he'd expected. His first was a skinny White girl with dull brown hair who, for some inexplicable reason, chose to jog between ten and ten-thirty nightly around the downtown canal. But her actions were inexplicable not only because she was jogging the moderately lit three miles around the canal in the dark of night alone, but because she appeared to be maybe one-hundred pounds even she filled all of her pockets with wrecking balls. Her lack of weight made her that much easier to overwhelm. Ben hid among shrubs along steps that ran perpendicular to the canal. It was the girl's exit route – always. When she got close enough, he exploded quickly from the brush, delivered a bone jarring karate chop to her throat before she could scream, and hit her with a left cross that knocked her out instantly. He was out of the brush, and had her in a large laundry bag and over his shoulder before she hit the landing. The steps led between two buildings in the Canal Square apartment complex, to the parking lot, and onto MLK Street just across from the Madame Walker Building. Ben chose today to kill the girl because it was the first time he'd been able to secure the first space at the edge of the no parking area. It took him two hours to get the space, and another two for the girl to come out for her jog. Ben's was one of the few houses among the Flanner House Homes that had an attached garaged. He'd made room for the stolen car. He furiously raped and sodomized the skinny White girl until she bled from every orifice. He stabbed her sixteen times before dumping her dead body into Fall Creek near 10th Street.

He and Relaine spent the following morning having big fun flirting while battling to conceal the fact that they were developing a relationship.

Victim number four was the short, fat, frumpy troll with stringy dirty blond hair and a face like the late Strom Thurmond. She was one of the numerous fist key grippers he'd noticed exiting the Gateway building at 10th and Illinois. The strange thing was that Ben had dismissed her as he'd done all others. But, apparently, his alter ego hadn't dismissed her at all. Now that Ben and his alter ego clearly shared conscious minds. She had to die.

Ben had to do mild surveillance on the troll, but his alter ego had all of the exits covered. The troll had the same routine. She left work at 5:30 pm, drove north on Illinois and stopped at that tiny enclave of businesses just south of Westfield Blvd. at the quite expensive liquor store and bought a pint of Johnny Walker scotch. She lived on a street just east of Illinois between Westfield and Kessler in a four bedroom tri-level house with her husband, a retired commercial airline pilot who was a veteran of over fifty years of smoking and was driven to be on oxygen by chronic emphysema. Frumpy had a good system of care for him, though. One of her daughters and her two children lived with them. The daughter worked nights three days per week. She was gone every Wednesday, and this Wednesday was no exception.

Ben waited until the house was dark. He knew that the kids were in bed by nine, and that Frumpy usually polished off the last drop of scotch by ten. Her husband was lights out no later than eleven. Ben made his move at eleven thirty. He entered the house via the rear patio door. It surprised him how people – especially White people – felt secure with a lock that could be broken by a grasshopper. Frumpy was quite a bit harder to subdue than the skinny jogger. Even though she had been sleeping, she was about five foot five, rocketing toward two-hundred pounds, and still drunk. Normally, a woman like her wouldn't even trigger a tingle from his penis, but there was something about violence that turned his dick into a flagpole. He got the duct tape onto her mouth first thing, wrestled with her for a few minutes before beating her senseless, slammed his dick into her one hundred times, sodomized her with her bowling trophy that she'd kept on her dresser, and then plunged his knife into her throat, nearly decapitating her. Out of respect for her grandchildren, he didn't turn the slaying into a bloodbath.

The next day, Relaine asked Ben if she could come by his place after work. He was feeling better than he had in years, otherwise he likely would've declined her request. They had a couple of drinks, talked, and then Relaine kissed him. He loved her restrained aggressiveness. They made out for half an hour, and when Ben moved his hands beneath her t-shirt, she let him fondle her for about a minute, and then broke away from him.

"I'm sorry," she said. "I'm not really ready. I'm really sorry."

"Don't be sorry," Ben answered. "The only way I know how far I can go is when I'm stopped."

Relaine knew at that moment that the next time they got together she was going to fuck him to within an inch of his life.

Ben's next victim was to be the tall, voluptuous, red haired woman from the Stutz Building. The one who'd feigned walking up Senate Ave., only to double back to her true destination, the parking lot, in order to avoid him, and stopped to talk to a homeless White man on the way back. She was a sales rep from one of the companies in the Stutz Building, so she was easy to follow. But there was a big problem. She was, by far, the most conscientiously careful person he'd ever seen in his life. She never took stairwells, rarely climbed on an elevator alone, parked her car almost exclusively where it could be seen from the street, left the gym only with two partners and then drove them to their respective vehicles, kept the family vehicles and the home where she lived with her husband and two small children protected with security systems that would make the Federal Bank green with envy, and she had once avoided a Black man who had nothing on his mind but to get some liquor in his system as soon as possible. He couldn't kill her that night.

Ben was a bit nervous the next evening as he drove over to Relaine's house. The news in Indy was dominated by the rash of rape/murders with. He felt good about the fact that his alter ego had schooled him on how to tie a condom around his penis beforehand to save time and effort, and to avoid leaving seminal DNA. But the fact that he'd been unable to kill the tall redhead bothered him the most. Things were getting hot in Indy, and he knew that in order to continue his spree, he needed to either: stop for a long time, move far away, or change his MO. Relaine's deep, sensuous kiss as a greeting at her door warmly calmed him.

"I didn't fix dinner, but I made some nachos and I've got plenty of booze," she smiled.

"I'm falling in love with you more every day," he said, the urge still building deep inside his soul.

"Fuck you Ben," she laughed. "Have a seat on the sofa." She went into the kitchen, and returned with a tray of nachos, two ice cold Bud Lights, and a fifth of Jose Cuervo tequila with two shot glasses. She showed him a stack of DVD's.

"I'll watch whatever you want to watch," he said. He'd downed two shots of tequila, and three swigs of beer before the FBI warning flared up on the screen.

"Slow down, partner," Relaine cautioned. "I don't want you passing out before the festivities begin."

"Don't worry, baby. If there's any passing out tonight, it won't be because of drinking."

The movie hadn't even run thirty minutes before Ben and Relaine were literally trying to suck out each other's souls. Ben's erection was almost painful as he was allowed to paw her like a horny tiger beneath her t-shirt. But it wasn't her he truly desired. He couldn't stop thinking about the tall redhead he'd missed killing the night before. It was she that he wanted to pound away at until she bled from her rectum. It was she that he wanted to use the knife in his car to cut the bloody cross into her pussy. And, right now, he couldn't help but to wonder whether or not Relaine was a good candidate for changing his MO, since he wanted to kill too much to stop killing, and he was too poor to move away. He was very confused. He wondered whether or not Relaine told anybody that he was coming over tonight. He grabbed her ass, and ground his pelvis onto her as he tried to choke her with his tongue. He needed to do something and do it quickly.

"Whoa, Whoa, slow down big player," Relaine gasped.

"Sorry. It's just that it's been a while since I've been with a woman."

"How long?"

"Too long."

Relaine giggled.

"What's so funny?"

"I just can't imagine a smart, good looking man like you going "too long" without being with a woman. You want another beer?"

"I'd love one," Ben answered as he poured himself another shot.

Relaine went to the kitchen and came back with two open beers. Ben took the beer from her and gulped it almost dry. The entire time he was thinking about how he could kill her tonight. He didn't want to do it, but his alter ego owned his soul now. He'd make powerful love to her, find a reason to leave, or maybe even just sneak out while she slept. His murder kit was in his vehicle. He'd wait an hour or so, and then return to do the deed.

"Are you okay, Ben?" Relaine asked. Her eyes were so soft, so warm, and so caring.

He couldn't do it. She cared for him. The others were hated strangers. But then, he felt a boiling in his belly that seemed to turn into a rock. He became extremely dizzy. His vision became blurred.

He could barely move. Relaine got up. She pulled the coffee table off of the throw rug below it. She then pulled Ben onto the rug. He could hear the crinkling of plastic below it. She pushed the corners of the sofa, one at a time, back about an inch, reached beneath the middle cushion where it seemed only minutes earlier that they were about to make love, and brandished a dagger. She straddled him at his knees, and then pulled him up by his neck so that he could feel her hot breath on his face.

"I really like you, Ben. But I have to do this." She plunged the knife deep into his gut, and twisted it. He couldn't scream. The Succynolcoline she'd bought from an old friend in Gary had paralyzed his muscles. She gently lowered his head to the floor, and then stabbed him twenty seven times in short forceful thrusts so that little if any of his blood would escape past the rug. She then dragged his bloody dead body into her back yard. She'd spent much of the day preparing the four foot hole. She wrapped him up, secured him with duct tape, rolled him into the hole, covered his body with lime, and buried him. She went inside, showered, and waited until three in the morning to drive his car about a half mile away. On her walk back, she thought to herself: "It wasn't nearly as good as I thought it was going to be."

HOUSE NIGGA'

A Short Story

By

E. Marvin Neville

Jonas Simpson strode slowly down the walk. He'd dreamed about making the walk for nearly eighteen months, and now it was like a nightmare where he was trying to escape a threat, and his legs were mired in drying cement. That all changed once he saw ex-wife Marla waiting for him in the parking lot.

He climbed into Marla's car. "Thanks for coming," he said.

"Well, no matter what you've done, I couldn't leave you hanging," she smiled.

"You make it sound like I killed somebody."

"You did. You murdered my love for you when you cheated with that White meth-head."

"And we're off to a good start."

"I know. Where're you going?"

"There's a halfway house on Twenty-second and Capitol."

"You make sure that you call WIS tomorrow. Divorced or not, I don't want you to go back to prison."

Washington Inventory Service was a company that specialized in inventories, and supplying jobs for the legally challenged. It was a far cry from where he'd come.

Jonas had been a chef for as long as he could remember, well before he'd gone to culinary school. He simply loved to cook. But, more importantly, he loved for diners to enjoy his work. He'd started as a short order cook part time in high school, continued as he worked his way through culinary school, and fought off offers from five states in the Midwest before he was able to secure financing for a restaurant of his own. The restaurant had been on the edge of downtown Indy, and it had been wildly successful. But it all started to fall apart when he hooked up with Kim.

Kim had been hired as a waitress, and even though Jonas had dated pretty White girls before marrying Marla, Kim mesmerized him with her thick petite-ness, blue-grey eyes, and funny wit and charm. In less than two months, she'd persuaded him to try meth. By month six, nearly all of his disposable income targeted the purchase of it.

Two days after his release, Jonas started work at WIS. He hated it. Not because of the work, that he liked. Counting merchandise in retail stores was just challenging enough to keep him sane. WIS paid eight dollars per hour to start. Most workers worked between twenty and thirty hours per week. It was the kind of place where people who really didn't want to work went to make enough cash to buy fuel for their vehicles, weed and liquor, or the occasional Big Mac.

A few weeks into his work for WIS, he met a brother and sister from North Carolina. He wouldn't have given them a second look but for the girl's eyes. They were the same blue-gray color as Kim's. It was almost scary. Her brother's name was Brother, and her name was Sister. Most of the WIS employees not only thought that their names were weird, they also thought that – because of the closeness of Sister and Brother – that were having sex. Jonas could understand how they would think that. The two did seem to cling on one another like two night crawlers having sex.

Sister was hard to get to know. She was polite, and quite sweet, but nobody seemed to be able to crack her shell. She was like a spy – hiding in plain sight. But Jonas got to know them both quite unexpectedly.

The crew had just completed a job at the Lowe's near eighty-sixth and Michigan Road.

"I've got a fifth of Bacardi Gold waiting for me," Jonas exclaimed.

"So do we," Brother laughed. Sister smiled, but looked a bit embarrassed.

Brother then suggested that Jonas come over to their place to share some of theirs. Normally, Jonas would've declined. After all, he barely knew them. But he accepted because Sister had been so cold toward him, he thought he might find out why. And because if he was drinking their Bacardi, he wasn't drinking his own.

After a few drinks, and a couple of blunts for the siblings (Jonas knew that drug use would land him back in jail if it showed up on his urinalysis), they all three opened up about their lives. The duo had grown up in North Carolina. When their parents divorced, their mother gained custody. She'd freely passed down her boozing and drug use to her children purely by example. When she decided to leave the state of North Carolina for Indiana with her pot dealing boyfriend, her ex-husband was ready and able to take in his two progeny. Brother was twelve, and Sister was ten.

By his thirteenth birthday, Brother was as good at stealing cars and burgling as thieves about whom movies had been made, and Sister had smelled the stink of her father's breath and felt the hot pain of his penis jamming inside of her only days after moving in with him. She was hurt, scared, but mostly very angry. But she was powerless, as was Brother.

Dear old dad made a small fortune coercing his son to steal, and pimping his daughter out to scum. Unfortunately, he spent it as fast as he made it, using drugs, gambling, and trying to be Mr. Big Shot of Appalachia. At age sixteen, Brother ran away, and took Sister with him.

They spent a few weeks on the street, and then were picked up by the police trying to steal food. Before the authorities could even call their father, Sister cried rape. There was little proof of the accusations, so as the authorities tried to build a case against him, he died in a suspicious fire, and the duo ended up separately in foster care. They were too old to be kept together.

Brother struggled in foster care. He couldn't seem to shake his thieving ways. Sister, on the other hand, flourished. Her grades in school exploded to straight A's. She took part in numerous extracurricular activities, and seemed destined for college. But there was only one thing that she wanted to do in life, and that was to reunite with Brother.

She'd kept herself safe, for the most part. She'd been done with men from the moment that her own father screwed her like a five-dollar whore. She not only excelled academically, but she came to accept the fact that women were much less of an emotional threat. And, that they knew more about what it took to please a woman sexually than any man would ever know. She went straight lesbian.

By the time she found Brother, he'd become the carbon copy of their father – except for the way he treated women. He was attractive and personable, but he concerned himself more with getting high using somebody else's money. She did her best to keep him out of jail. She worked dead-end jobs, while he worked as much as he could stand, and stole only where and when she told him. They survived.

They found their mother in Indianapolis. She and her boyfriend were doing far less than prospering, but their mother did feel a bit of remorse for having left them with their father. To make up for it, she convinced her boyfriend to let them move into a mildly crappy house in Haughville that he owned. The house had been left to him by his parents, and he really wasn't much of a landlord. He, too, loved to party. But the house was pretty secure, so it wasn't in horrible shape when Sister and Brother moved into it. Sister led Brother through a few minor thefts in order to pay to bring the place up to code, and then one of her female lovers helped to get the jobs at WIS. On their second day, they met Jonas. It was a meeting that would end up changing all of their lives.

Jonas, Sister, and Brother were all well above being drunk while having a great, sharing time. "It's time for me to go, guys," Jonas proclaimed.

"Dude, you should stay here for the night," Brother responded.

"What're you talking about?" Sister said, switching from happily drunk to uncontrollably angry. "We don't know this motherfucker!"

"She's right," Jonas returned. "I really should be going."

"Thanks for the dinner," Sister offered.

"Hold up, sis. You can kick the asses of everybody I know. I think the both of us can take this guy if necessary," Brother slurred.

"I think you just gave me even more reason to leave," Jonas smiled. He got up, a bit unstably.

"No, dude, I'm just saying that a guy who can cook up a dinner like you did with the bullshit we had in the fridge can't be that dangerous."

"So you're saying I'm gay, and that there's no way that a faggot could kill anybody?"

"No, man, I'm just saying that you seem cool to me, and I don't want you to get popped after we've had such a good time."

"Thanks, but I have to agree with your sister. I...."

Sister interrupted. "Enough! You can stay. There's a mattress in the third bedroom. It's kind of skanky, and we don't have linens for it, but you can sleep on it if you like," she said.

Jonas wanted to be powerful, and leave the house. But he was pretty drunk. He agreed.

Sister was right about the mattress. It didn't matter. He dropped onto the mattress fully clothed, and didn't realize that he'd fallen asleep until he awoke a few hours later. He was still buzzing, but he was also hungry. He sneaked out of the house, bought, and prepared breakfast. The smell itself awoke the siblings. It was eight o'clock in the morning. Only Jonas was used to being up so early, except, in prison, it hadn't been by choice. There was no work that day, so they all ate, drank, and the siblings smoked. Jonas was ready to leave by noon.

"Hold up, Jonas," Brother said.

"Now what's wrong?" Sister asked.

"Listen. I'm just saying that it might be a good idea for Jonas to move in here with us."

"What the fuck are you talking about?"

"Are you clean, Jonas?" Brother asked.

"I'm scared to sit on the toilet seat in your bathroom. So I hovered above it like a debutante at a biker bar this morning."

"What the fuck does that mean?" Sister asked Jonas Angrily.

Brother jumped in. "Look, sis, we're all struggling here. And we all have something to offer. Jonas strikes me as the kind of guy who understands that."

"I haven't left the house yet," Jonas responded.

"Okay. Hear me out, sis. If he moves in, all three of us are spending less money. He cooks and cleans, you and I still split the rent, but he splits the utilities and food, and he cooks and cleans for us all."

"That's insane, Brother," Sister said.

"Only if I have to clean your rooms," Jonas returned.

"Don't make me slap you, Jonas."

"I'm not scared of you, Sister, even though you do have a weird name."

Sister smiled. "I'm not sure about this. We don't know you."

"Nor do I know you two. But we all do work for WIS."

The three laughed.

"When can you move in, Jonas?" Brother asked.

"I have to be out of my room before the end of the week, or another week's rent is due."

Jonas was in before sunset, and he brought his rum with him. They had another great party.

Things turned out to really be quite good in the house in Haughville. Jonas controlled every room other than the sibling's bedrooms, and he'd quickly developed a system to keep them clean that rendered both of them oblivious to the moderate amount of work required from him to keep the house apparently spotless. All three ate well, and almost never needed to eat fast food. And the bills were so much easier to pay.

Jonas mostly kept to himself, with weekly forays into the bed of his ex-wife. Sister had a girlfriend who stayed over a good deal, and Brother was hardly ever at home. They were like a family of highly dysfunctional individuals who'd found an unusual way of functioning. It didn't take long for Sister to warm up to Jonas as if she were a combination of father, brother, and friend to him. He was the most amazing person she'd every known.

Marla felt extraordinarily guilty for the Wednesday forays with her ex-husband – the cheating on her boyfriend – but she'd never stopped loving Jonas. She kept Jonas distant, but yet she couldn't wait for their time together.

Jonas loved his time with Marla. But he couldn't help but to feel that she was only experiencing residual feelings. And as much as he wanted to be with her, there was still an ocean's worth of uncertainty.

Jonas walked into a small party at home after a WIS trip to St. Louis that hadn't included Sister and Brother. He'd been gone for three days. He made nachos for the group of four women and two men. Sister scuttled quickly up to her room with her girlfriend once the nachos were gone, and Brother followed with one of the remaining girls shortly thereafter. That left Jonas alone with a fairly skanky, young White girl who was so drunk that he couldn't see her eyes. He offered to bring her down bedding for the sofa, but she preferred to go up to his room with him. He didn't hesitate. He was horny.

The next morning, Sister seemed angry with him. He didn't understand. Her anger seemed jealousy based.

"What's wrong?" Jonas asked.

"What do you mean? There's nothing wrong."

"Well, you've treated me like an STD all morning."

"Maybe that's because you are an STD," Sister sneered.

"I'm not even going to dignify that with a response."

"Why did you fuck Mindy last night?"

"Well, everybody else was fucking, why not us?"

"Please tell me you used a condom."

"I have a case of them in my room, Sister. What's going on here?"

She dropped her head. "Nothing, Jonas. I just worry about you."

"I appreciate that, baby. But I'm a big boy."

Brother came down the stairs. "What's going on, guys?" he asked blearily.

"Nothing," Sister said. She stormed upstairs.

Jonas didn't see Sister again until that evening. He'd slept most of the day, but was cooking dinner when she walked through the front door. She came into the kitchen, and got a beer. Neither of them said a word. He could live with the silence. It was being unaware of what was wrong with her that bothered him.

Sister had gone to her room. Brother wasn't home. Jonas took her a plate of steamy chicken stir fry. He knocked. "I've got dinner for you, Sister," he exclaimed. He was met with silence. "We live and work together, babe. We're going to have to speak eventually."

"Come in, Jonas," Sister moaned.

Jonas slowly opened the door, balancing two plates of food on his right arm like a tremendously experienced waiter. Sister smiled. "You never cease to amaze me," she said.

"Then why are you so angry with me?"

She sighed as he handed her a plate. "It's not you. It's me."

"That sounds like a sitcom."

"I know, Jonas. It's just that, other than Brother, you're the only man I've ever known who seems to be what a man should be. I mean, you listen to what I have to say, and I've never seen a twinkle of judgment in your eyes. You moved in here, and you made everything better. It's like you're related to us. I just hated seeing you with someone who's probably a lot like Kim."

Cement putty over Jonas' eyes couldn't have stopped the tears from streaming. "I really appreciate that, Sister."

"I know," she returned. They stared at each other for about five seconds, and then he took a chance. He slammed his mouth onto hers, praying that she wouldn't draw away from him. She didn't. They tried to devour each other. Their plates of stir fry clanked to the floor as they ripped off each others clothes. Kissing hard, they stared into each others eyes as Jonas plunged inside of Sister. Once he penetrated her, he flipped over onto his back, carrying her with Him, and then spun her and pulled her back to his belly so that they both faced the ceiling. He pumped slowly, but intensely inside of her as he fondled her clitoris with his left hand and her breasts with his right hand. He licked her neck, tongued her ear, and kissed her until saliva dripped down their cheeks. It took less than fifteen minutes for her to explode into a thrashing ecstasy the likes of which he'd never even seen on a porn video. Sister ripped herself away from him onto the floor in the corner of the room, and whimpered between near violent quivers. Jonas approached her.

"Get away from me," Sister screamed.

"What's wrong?" he asked

"Get away from me, and get the fuck out of my room!"

"What did I do?"

"Go!"

Jonas followed her order. He ran to his room naked. He was feeling extraordinarily vulnerable. He almost peed himself when his bedroom door swung open. It was Sister. Tears flowed down her face like a busted dam. She slammed the door closed, and locked it. She dove onto Jonas, and thrust her mouth onto his penis. She pumped it as if she were trying to extract his soul – tears streaming from her eyes, and mucus flowing from her nose. After he exploded into her mouth, and she sucked and swallowed everything that she could, she released him. Blood dripped from his penis, and droplets wavered on her lips. She gave him a look he'd never seen in a human being before, and then hustled out of his bedroom.

Jonas was almost scared to face her the following morning. He walked on eggshells as he prepared breakfast. Sister stepped into the kitchen, and smiled at him. She said nothing. He wanted to talk, but he was still a bit fearful. She turned and looked at him as she poured herself a cup of coffee. "I know. That wasn't supposed to happen," she said.

"I'm not sure what to think, Sister."

"Do you still love your wife?"

Jonas sighed. "I think you know the answer to that question."

"You know. I've had a lot of sex. The overwhelming majority of it was crushing and numbing. But I've got to say that loving you last night was astronomically the best sex that I've ever had in my life."

"It was the best for me, too, Sister."

"Please. You don't have to say that."

"I bled into your mouth, and you didn't even blink."

"But you still love your wife, right?"

Jonas could do nothing but nod. Marla was still his girl.

"We'll never speak of this, Jonas. We'll forget about it."

"I'll never speak of it, but I'll never forget it."

Over the next week, Jonas and Sister were as friendly as friends could be, and their searing night of passion was becoming increasingly obscured.

One night, Jonas was watching the late night news. Usually, he avoided the news like a prairie dog avoided coyotes. Jonas' mouth dropped when he saw the lead story.

Two people, a man and a woman, had been stabbed to death on Indianapolis' east side. That in and of itself wasn't so profound. People were murdered on the east side like mail deliveries. The shock was that the victims were Kim and her cohort – the one's who'd robbed him and caused him to become an ex-convict. They'd underestimated him thinking that he wouldn't risk prison time by squealing to the police.

Jonas felt bad. He'd wanted Kim to feel pain for betraying him – for drugs no less, but he'd forgiven them both long ago. There was a knock at the door. It was Sister. "Did you see the news?" she asked as she walked in and plopped onto his bed.

"Yeah," Jonas responded solemnly.

"Why aren't you happy?"

"Two people died."

"They ripped you off, and made you go to prison," Sister returned indignantly.

"No. I made me go to jail. I don't think I would've ever done what they did to me, but I was buying and doing lots of meth, Sister."

"Touché, sir," Sister smiled. "Is there anything I can do to help ease your pain for your friends?"

Jonas took Sister by the back of her head, and slammed her mouth onto his. Daylight, and four condoms later, the two passed out – no strings attached.

The following Wednesday, Jonas called Marla to find out at which hotel they would meet. She'd been a stickler for changing hotels so that they wouldn't establish a pattern. "Come on to the house," Marla said.

"Excuse me?"

"Come to the house."

"Our house?"

"That's where I live."

"I don't understand, Marla."

"I broke up with Morgan about six weeks ago. I waited to see how I felt about doing it, and how he would react to the breakup before I told you."

"Why would you tell me?"

"You're still my best bet, Jonas," Marla said through tears.

"Your best bet?"

"We're both dive bombing to our forties, Jonas. I make a great living, and you'll be back on top before you know it. I want a family, and I still want to make that family with you."

"Then why did you divorce me?"

"You're cheating a felon, I'm a lawyer."

"What's different now?"

"You're the felon I want to raise a family with."

Jonas and Marla made universe creating love, and that was putting it mildly.

The next day, Jonas informed Sister and Brother of his new plans. Marla had even set him up with an interview for chef at a brand new downtown restaurant. Neither of them expected much, but it was a start. The siblings were ecstatic for Jonas. They decided to throw an impromptu going away party for him.

As was normal for the get-togethers held in the house in Haughville, all of the guests were friends of Sister and brother. As usual, Jonas' nachos disappeared like twenty-dollar bills in a casino. He went into the kitchen to bring out more. Out of respect for him, the meth users were disappearing one to two at a time to smoke. But he could smell it better than he could smell his own farts. While Jonas was in the kitchen, one of the partiers laughed.

"What's so funny?" Brother asked.

"I don't know, man. This is the first time I've smoked in here on over six months."

"And your point is what?" Sister asked.

"I'm just saying that ever since Jonas has been living here, we can't party here."

"Come on, dude. We told you months ago that for him to live here...." Brother said.

"....And makes the food that you enjoy so much," Sister finished Brother's sentence.

"....We agreed to not do meth around him. And he was right, as far as I know. He's done nothing but good in this house," Brother said. "We're proud of him, and we're even happier that he's on his way back to his wife."

"We love him," Sister proclaimed.

"And he loves us," Brother added.

"I got that," the guest responded. "But what I'm saying is that he's the only black person here."

"And that means what?" Sister asked.

"Well, that he's like a House Nigger."

"A what?" Sister asked.

"You know, he's serving all of the White people in the house, like in the slavery days."

The room was so quiet that chirping crickets could be heard from Zionsville. Sister sprang into action. She judo chopped the offender hard in the throat, causing him to choke. She grabbed his trailer park length hair, pulled him to his feet, twisted his arm behind his back, and marched him into his kitchen. Sister forced the offender to apologize to Jonas for something Jonas hadn't even heard spoken.

It was Thursday, but Jonas wanted more than anything in the world to impregnate Marla that night. He craved her. He was back, and better, and smarter, than ever. But a knock at the door interrupted the master plan.

Marla's ex-boyfriend, Michael, showed up. She tried to keep him at the front door, but Jonas thought that it was a good idea for all three to be outside.

"So this is the looser you dumped me for?" Michael exclaimed.

"Dude, you don't even know me," Jonas answered calmly.

"I know you're a convict."

"That's ex-convict."

Michael turned to Marla. "You've been fucking this guy, haven't you?" he screamed.

"Michael, please. You don't understand. I never stopped loving him," Marla pledged.

"So you used me until he got out of prison?"

"No, Michael. I just didn't think I loved him any more."

"Why didn't you tell me that when you dumped me?"

"Look at you now, Michael. It's been six weeks. I'll bet you've watched my house ever since then?"

"I love you Marla."

"No, you just love the idea of me being yours. That's not what a man does."

"What do you know about being a man? You're a woman."

"I've got to throw him some props one that one, baby," Jonas smiled.

"Ain't nobody talking to you, convict."

"Look, player. When I got the divorce papers from her in prison, I wanted to hurt somebody. But I didn't, and not just because I would've gotten more time."

"It's time for you to shut up, and leave me and Marla alone," Michael said, and looked with loving derangement toward Marla. "I know we can work this out, baby."

"I'm sorry, Michael," Marla said tearfully.

"That's not going to happen, Michael," Jonas said.

Michael looked down, and then lifted his head, and threw a punch that he was certain Jonas wasn't ready for. He was wrong. Jonas ducked the punch, and slammed a straight right into Michael's solar plexus. When Michael doubled over, Jonas rose quickly, banging the back of his head onto Michael's mouth, knocking out two teeth, and dropping him to the ground. Jonas told Marla to call the police. Michael got to his feet, and staggered to his car. "This ain't over," he proclaimed as he peeled away.

Marla gave Jonas the new keys to the house, and the new alarm code before he left for his interview the next morning.

It turned out to not be an interview at all. When the restaurateur found out that the Marla was the ex-wife of the man who'd owned the restaurant where he'd solidified huge business deals before Jonas' fall, he'd asked Marla to make the introduction. He wanted Jonas to run his mostly seafood establishment from the moment he'd first dreamed about it. Jonas was hired before he'd even walked in the door. He was explosively happy.

After leaving the restaurant, he called Marla. "Why didn't you tell me I already had the job?"

"Because you would've thought that I got the job for you. You know how you are, Jonas. You hate help."

"No. I love help. I just never knew that I did. Okay, I hated help until now."

"You've always had help, Jonas."

"I promise you that, as soon as I can, I'm going to strike back out on my own. But, right now, I'm about to start to make a hundred grand a year doing what I love, and I'm happy with that. You're the cream that makes me understand just how fortunate I am."

"So am I going to see you tonight?"

"Michael can't keep me away."

136

"I've got a surprise for you."

"The phone will be sitting on my chest as I rest in preparation."

When Jonas got to Haughville, the house was empty. He wanted to share his joy with his young roommates. Instead, he spent the next few hours packing up most of his belongings, and cooking dinner for Sister and Brother.

Marla called Jonas at dusk. She apologized for being so late.

Jonas pulled up in front of their house. The only light on in the house was in the bedroom. Jonas became even more excited about his surprise. He used his keys, and the alarm code.

Jonas called out to Marla. Yes, she was expecting him, but he didn't want to scare her to death. Jonas rushed up to Marla's bedroom, and walked through the door. He almost fainted when he saw her bound and gagged in a chair at the far side of the room. Immediately, he realized that he had put himself in an extremely life threatening position. As badly as he wanted to rush to Marla, he knew that he could do nothing if he was dead. Jonas dropped to the floor on his back. He needed to see what was going on around him. Nothing moved. He prayed that there wasn't a gun in the room, unless Marla could shoot it from her mouth. It seemed that nobody was in the room, but Marla groaned frantically. It was obvious that somebody was there. Before Jonas could make his next decision, that person came out from the darkness. Jonas all but peed himself.

Sister walked in from a dark corner holding a serrated knife that was large enough to kill and gut a rhinoceros. "Hi, baby," she said.

"What's up, Sister?"

"I'm just taking care of business."

"Business?"

"I took care of your enemies, Jonas."

"My enemies?"

"Kim, and her stupid boyfriend."

"You killed them?"

"It was easy. I waited for them, just like I waited for your ex-wife here. I wasn't expecting you, though, Jonas. Why are you here?"

"Don't do this, Sister."

Sister screamed. "They hurt you." She looked at Marla. "She hurt you. Once she's gone, it'll be just you and me. That's the way it's supposed to be."

"I thought you didn't care, Sister."

"I care only about you."

"What about brother?"

"He cares about whatever I tell him to care about. You fucked me as if you lived inside of my soul, Jonas."

"Fucking doesn't make a good, lasting relationship."

"Don't treat me like an idiot, Jonas. You know there was way more than physicality. I'm your girl, you're my man. Together, we can rule the world."

"I don't want to rule the world."

"Yes you do. We're going to start now."

Sister put the knife to Marla's throat, and commanded Jonas to undress. He did. Sister's plan was to fuck him right in front of the only woman he'd ever truly loved, and then kill her. Sister was prepared to make the scene look like a murder/suicide if she had to. She pulled up her skirt, and cut off her panties seductively. She walked over to the bed, and climbed on. She had to use her knife fist for leverage in order to climb on top of him. Jonas quickly grabbed her right wrist with his left hand. She, too, was quick. She tapped the blade toward his wrist as far as she could. The blade was sharp. He could feel it cutting his flesh. Still, he was able to keep his grip. Sister made him woozy with three pounding left handed blows to his face. And then something truly bizarre happened.

Jonas was struggling for the lives of him and Marla when Sister's vagina slipped onto his rock-hard penis. Jonas found himself to be quite upset that in the fight to save lives, he had the most powerful erection of his life. Sister caught him hard with another left before he could grab her left wrist. He held onto her, waiting for the cobwebs to clear out of his head, as she rode him like a racehorse. Marla became furious.

She bounced herself over to the bed, and with all the might she could muster, launched herself onto it. She managed to knock Sister off balance just enough to allow Jonas to get on top her. He slammed three stiff rights onto her jaw, breaking his middle and ring fingers. Sister was knocked out. Jonas scrambled to his wife, begging her forgiveness as he unbound her. Suddenly, Sister sprang to life. She dove across the bed at them. Jonas felt stupid for not removing the knife from her hand. He dove on Marla, toppling them both to the floor, and dodging Sister. Sister's head slammed into the wall, creating a hole that nearly engulfed her entire head. Jonas kicked the knife out of her hand, ripped out the phone cord, and tied her hands behind her without even checking her for life.

Twenty minutes had passed since the attack. Sister was carted out to the ambulance, handcuffed to the rail. She was unconscious. The paramedics treated the Simpson's. Marla was mostly just shaken, but Jonas was going to go to the emergency room for his hand. Marla walked over to him. He hung his head. "I'm sorry, baby," he said.

Marla shook her head. "You know anybody who can fix that hole in the wall?" she asked.

Jonas raised his head, laughed, and then kissed his wife. It was strange how good a deep kiss from the love of one's life tasted after surviving a deadly attack.

THE RIVER PROMENADE FANTASY

A Short Story

By

E. Marvin Neville

Martin Morris trudged his way into his house on Brooks Lane, a stone's throw from historic Crispus Attucks in downtown Indianapolis after his daily after work five-mile run. As he walked in, his live-in girlfriend of five years, Regina Chatman, screamed out to him. "What took you so long?"

"What're you talking about?"

"I know how long it takes for you to make your run! You're two hours late!"

"I called you at work, Regina. I left a voice message telling you that I had to work a ten hour day," Martin sighed.

"I didn't get a voice message, Martin," she answered.

"Did you check them?"

"You're really pissing me off now."

"I left it, Regina. If you don't know what happened, I don't have a chance of knowing."

"Martin, if I ever find out you're cheating on me, you know I'll kill you and the bitch you're fucking."

"I heard all one-hundred thirty seven thousand times you've said that before."

"Don't get smart, Martin."

Martin sighed again as he made his way to the shower. He truly loved Regina regardless of her need to be abrasive. She was good for him, even though she acted as though her job as a legal secretary at a downtown law firm was better than his job as a forklift driver at the Target Distribution Center near Indianapolis International Airport. He earned six dollars per hour more than did she, but that didn't matter to her. And, in a way, it didn't matter to him. She managed the finances like the CEO of a Fortune 500 company, and even though he hated being on a seventy-five dollar per week allowance, he loved the fact that their credit cards were at a five percent balance, and they had a decent amount of funds in their savings. Martin had never been very good at managing money. Regina made sure that there was always money available.

Martin had a ten-year old son whose mother Martin had broken up with because he'd cheated on her with Regina. Regina made sure that Martin never had to go near a courthouse regarding child support, but she also never let it slip from her mind that he was capable of not only cheating, but cheating to an end of leaving her for another woman. Martin, on the other hand, wasn't a habitual cheater. He'd loved his son's mother, and then he fell in love with Regina. He wasn't a sophisticated guy. He met Regina at Black Expo 2003, at the job fair. They both liked their jobs, but they also wanted to explore their respective options.

The meeting of Martin and Regina seemed to be pure chance. He was buying a bottle of three-dollar Dasani water from a nearby dispenser, and she walked up telling him how he was wasting money when there was perfectly good fountain water less than one-hundred yards away. He argued his position that bottled water was less laden with bacteria and sediments. She argued that scientific research that she'd seen on TV stated that there was virtually no difference between the two, other than the cost. The battle had never ended between them. Regina was always crashing through walls while Martin built defenses against offenses. That dynamic created a strange kind of balance that neither of them could explain to outsiders. It was as if they really didn't want to be together, but they had to be together in order for their respective lives to work.

Their sex life was like a conduit to that dynamic. Neither of them were titans in the sack. Martin had decent penile resistance to ejaculation, but it was Regina who made their sex life good. It took ten minutes when she was on top of him and fifteen minutes doggy style – her preferred position – for her to orgasm. She was often embarrassed that she came so fast, and tried many times to hold off, which was typically male. Martin ran with the fumble every time. He was almost always free to pump away at her, knowing she'd already been sexually satisfied.

Even better, Regina was infertile because she'd had one too many abortions in her youth. The only reason to worry about protection was because of STD's, and they'd been together long enough that, even when she vehemently accused Martin of cheating, she never asked him to use a condom. But he did wonder whether or not her constant anger with him was rooted in her inability to have children, in addition to the fact that she'd had so many failed relationships. It didn't matter much now. Martin Morris and Regina Chatman had a good balance. They owned both of their vehicles outright, and they were in route to owning their home in fifteen years or less. It was a good balance.

After dinner, Martin and Regina cleaned up the kitchen, showered together, went to bed and had their sex. Breathlessly, Regina mentioned that she wanted to travel to Chicago on the weekend after the Brickyard 400 NASCAR race at the end of July. She really wanted to go on the weekend of the race, but she didn't want to deal with any traffic. Martin liked the idea. He liked visiting Chicago. It was a great place to party and have fun, especially in the warm months of the year. "It's a date," he said. Regina smiled, turned over, and fell asleep almost immediately.

Martin got off work at his regular time the next day, and put yesterday's dinner in the oven at low temperature so that it would be ready for he and Regina by the time they both got home. Regina did almost all of the cooking. Martin made sure that the leftovers weren't ruined. He was good at that. He went for his run. He loved running. He'd run cross country in high school, and had even won a few races, but he was good enough at running to simply stay in shape, and reap the enjoyment. And enjoy it he did. He ran his way out of the Flanner House Homes on Brooks Lane, up Tenth Street between Wishard Hospital and Fall Creek, past the VA Hospital at Porto Allegre Street, and up New York Street toward the River Promenade. It was his usual route, and the River Promenade was his favorite part of the run.

The River Promenade was far and away the most beautiful part of Indy to Martin. When he and Regina first moved into the Flanner House Homes area, he ran the canal. It was a good run, but his problem with it was that there were so many beautiful White women, and, more importantly, so many couples who seemed to be so in love. That was a huge distraction for him. He loved Regina, but he never felt the love that he thought he saw between the couples that he encountered on his runs on the canal. At least he didn't think he had. He just didn't know. One thing that he did yearn for, though, was for that heavy hitting love – that love that wasn't just about efficiency. He wasn't stupid. He and Regina had an excellent relationship where feelings were secondary to a business model. That was a good thing. But he fantasized constantly about how it would feel to be head over heels in love – how the people he saw at the canal who cuddled, spoke softly to one another, and even simply held hands while walking together felt as they navigated the perilous waters of love. How did it feel to want to live for someone other than a direct blood relative? How did it feel to be willing to die for that person?

At the River Promenade, a half mile stretch of White River State Park that lied between the top of the White River Delta and the Indianapolis Zoo, with trees and foliage that rendered it beautiful without obscuring the view of downtown Indy, there were almost entirely exercisers. It was a terrific place for lovers, but only the lovers who were excruciatingly serious about exercising seemed to take advantage of it. There were mostly lone exercisers. It was perfect for Martin.

Martin was running past one of two River Promenade monuments when he saw something that nearly turned his heart into chicken noodle soup. A woman more beautiful than anything he'd ever seen in his life was running toward him from the opposite direction. He couldn't assign a nationality to her. She had the full roundness of a Negroid, the pointed sharpness of a Caucasoid, and the smooth darkness of a Mongoloid all combined into one being. Her hair was jet black, her eyes were large and perfectly set apart, the shape of her head was the stuff of artistic muse, and she had the nerve to have dimples. Her breasts were neither large nor small, and bounced joyfully despite her athletic bra, and her rear would never knock over buildings, but could certainly break windows. She was, by far, the perfect creation of a woman that he'd ever seen, and he saw her only briefly as they ran past each other. She smiled at him, and he smiled back. He couldn't help but to think that his smile belied the true vulnerability he felt as he glanced into her gorgeous brown eyes. He couldn't stop thinking about her.

Over the next seven days, Martin and the mystery woman passed each other at the exact same spot on their respective runs. She looked more beautiful each time he encountered her, and he decided that she would be his fantasy girl – the woman that he dreamed that he was head over heals in love with like the couples that he saw at the canal. He named her Jennifer. He didn't know why. It just seemed to be the right name.

That night, he closed his eyes and imagined that he was making love to Jennifer as he had sex with Regina. They'd been together for five years, and never had the sex between them been so intense. It launched past being efficient. Martin made love to Regina as if he were trying to prove himself for the first time. He was far from being a sex expert, but after their initial ten minutes, he still had an erection. They made love four times – each subsequent time more powerful than the time before. Regina was floored. She'd always loved making love to Martin because she cared so much about him, but that night spoke something to her that she'd never felt before carnally. He loved her. She'd been hurt so many times before him that it was hard to trust a man. For once, the man that she knew was good for the business of a relationship wanted her and only her. Her fourth orgasm was like a nuclear explosion. She couldn't have children, but she was ready to steal a child so that they could have a family. That was how much she'd fallen in true love with him that night.

The next day on his run, Martin saw Jennifer at the same spot on the River Promenade. She slowed down as she approached him. He stopped for her.

"How're you doing?" she asked.

"I've been better," he answered.

"Oh, stock answer."

Martin was transfixed by her deep brown eyes. "I guess you can say that," he said.

She extended her hand. "I'm Jennifer, Jennifer Nelson," she said.

Martin's knees buckled. "Pleased to meet you," he responded.

"Are you okay?"

"Yes, well, it's just that I've seen you over the last several days, and I decided that your name was Jennifer."

"You're good."

"I don't know about that. I did something that I know is wrong."

"What's that?"

"I can't tell you that."

"Why not?" Jennifer smiled.

"Because you'll think I'm crazy," Martin returned.

"I could never think that of you."

Martin's heart crashed for her to the point where he was ready to take the chance of never seeing her again. Her eyes were so engaging, and her body was so spectacular. "After the seventh time I saw you I imagined you as I made love to my girlfriend," he said. He was ready for Jennifer to sprint away.

"I took seven times," she smiled. "Was the loving good?"

"The best we've ever had," he answered, perplexed.

"Good," Jennifer said as she took off running. Martin watched her. She stopped, and turned around. "I'll see you tomorrow," she said, and then she turned and ran away.

Regina was all but crushed by Martin's lovemaking efforts that night. He even went so far as to give her the oral sex that he used to give her when they first began sleeping together. They both called in sick to work, and they screwed all day the next day. Their relation was starting to feel like what a marriage was supposed to feel like. Regina wondered whether or not Martin was going to pop the question. Martin wondered whether or not he could continue to make love to Regina while actually imagining another woman.

Regina was making dinner when he dressed for his run that day of hooky from work for both of them. She was so mellow. She encouraged him to go. She was certain of what she was going to get in bed after he returned from his run. She ended up getting what she expected and more, but Martin got something else from his run. Once again, he and Jennifer met at the Empire State Building monument on the River Promenade, but this time they both stopped and sat on the limestone. "What's wrong?" Martin asked.

"You were honest about you fantasizing about me with your girlfriend. I want to be honest about me and my former boyfriend," Jennifer said.

"You're so beautiful, Jennifer. It's not like I thought you didn't have a guy."

"That's not what I'm saying."

"What are you saying?"

Jennifer hesitated. "He tried to kill me," she said. Her eyes pierced his like a heated sword through ice.

"Why?"

"We had a fight after dinner at Appleby's in Broad Ripple, and he decided that we both should die. He drove off of the bridge at College over White River."

"He tried to kill you both?"

"Yes," Jennifer moaned. "But I swam out."

"Do you feel guilty that you lived?" Martin asked.

"Every single day of my life," she responded.

"It wasn't your fault."

"I know. All I wanted to do was to be in love so that I would want to give my life for that person."

"Did you feel that love?"

Jennifer smiled begrudgingly, got up, and started to run. She stopped running, turned, and looked at Martin. "You want to run together sometime?" she asked.

"We go different directions," Martin responded.

"I can change, Martin. I'll wait for you at the north entrance of the River Promenade tomorrow."

Martin ravaged Regina that night as if he'd just come home from eighteen months on the open sea. She said that she loved him as he rolled off of her. "I love you, too," he answered. He felt guilty. Did he love Regina, or did he love the fantasy that was Jennifer Nelson

The next day, Jennifer was waiting for Martin at the north entrance to the River Promenade. Her smiled melted him at the knees. Her teeth were so white, and her lips were so fully perfect. He was a dark skinned Black man, who wasn't ugly, but neither was he particularly good looking. Regina was cute. Her skin was caramel, and she had the biggest hazel eyes with long, natural lashes. She was a bit chunky, but Martin had always liked his women slightly overweight. But Jennifer was so perfect that he still found himself at a loss in determining her ethnicity. She joined him in the run. "You look kind of slow today," she smiled. "Did you make hot love with your girlfriend last night?"

"Thanks to you, it was the hottest yet."

"That's really sweet in a creepy kind of way."

"I know, but I've already admitted that you're my fantasy. Why avoid the awkwardness now?"

Suddenly, Jennifer slowed to a stop at the limestone monument of the Empire State Building, the Indiana State Capital, and The Washington DC Cathedral. They'd been carved into the wall that separated the trail from the hilltop of the White River Delta. There was just enough space before the slope for people to stand. Jennifer went in, and Martin followed. They were silent briefly. "Why are we stopping here?" Martin asked.

"Just look at it, Martin. It's so beautiful," Jennifer said of the spectacular view of the river as it wound its way towards the downtown Indy skyline.

"Yes, it is beautiful. But not nearly as beautiful as you."

Jennifer looked at Martin. He saw the universe in her eyes. There was sadness and joy. There was melancholy and ecstasy. There was intellect and emotion. A tear rolled slowly down her face, and then she shocked Martin by slamming her mouth onto his. Kissing her was as if he were a honeybee drawing nectar from a beautiful flower, except the flower had attacked him. He wouldn't have stopped even if he'd wanted to stop. They made out like hormone-driven teenagers. And even though the River Promenade was not exactly heavily traveled, the fact that were making out in public excited Martin even more. He had no idea what was to come.

Martin and Regina screwed so hard that night they rolled off of the bed, and crashed onto the floor. They both laughed like drunken debutantes. Martin knew that he was in emotional trouble. He loved both women unexplainably deeply

Martin met Jennifer again at the River Promenade. She ran with him to a carved monument only a few yards south of the Empire State Building carving. There was more land behind the sculpture that favored a stained glass church window, and was unnamed. She led him to the river side of the wall, slammed him against it, and pulled down both of their shorts while kissing him passionately. They were a perfect fit against the wall as she pounded at him fiercely. They shared the explosive orgasm. Martin had never experienced a simultaneous orgasm before.

Over the next few weeks, Martin alternated between Regina and Jennifer daily. The sex was vigorous, yet he never felt tired. Jennifer rented a tiny bungalow on Saucy St. across the street from the River Promenade, and apportioned it with only a sheet covered air mattress, and bathroom supplies for cleaning up after their trysts. She claimed that she lived far away, and that the little love shack made it easier for them to be together. Martin couldn't begin to even think of arguing.

Martin thought it kind of strange that Jennifer never mentioned the two of them striking out together, and neither did he broach the subject. But being between two women that he loved was driving him mad. He simply wasn't the kind of guy who played any kind of field. He was, and always had been, a one woman man. He was going to have to make a choice. But then, the choice was made for him.

Martin and Regina had just ended a night of near violent, multiply orgasmic lovemaking. Martin went right off to sleep. After all, it had been his fifth go round with two different women. Regina climbed out of bed. She was thirsty. She noticed that Martin's cell phone was lit up. There was a missed call. She hadn't heard it ring, but she had to acknowledge that their sex life had become so intensely wild that it was possible that their vigor had simply drowned out the ringing. She checked Martin's phone. The name Jennifer Nelson came up on the screen. Regina almost became infuriated, but she settled herself instead. Times between her and Martin had been so good. Perhaps there was an innocent explanation for the late night call from a female unknown to her. She decided to not ask, but to do a little investigating of her own. She started with the obvious move, and called the number for Jennifer Nelson on the caller ID. There was nothing but dead air on the other end. She tried several more times with the same results.

Over the next few days, Regina checked everything she could think of where Martin might hide damaging proof of infidelity. She checked the home computer, the lap top, his phone a dozen times, all of his clothing. There was no further reference to a Jennifer Nelson. She even took an afternoon off work to follow him from his job, to home, and on his run. She lost him at the River Promenade, and, fearing that he'd discover her tailing him, went home to wait for him. He came home on time, but she couldn't resist her natural instinct of distrust. "Who's Jennifer Nelson?" she asked.

Martin was caught so off guard that he thanked God that he wasn't facing Regina as he sat on the bed, removing his running clothes. He gathered himself quickly. "Who?" he asked.

"Jennifer Nelson."

Martin quickly realized what to do. "I don't recognize that name," he said.

"Well, it was on your phone a few nights ago."

"Did she leave a message?"

"No."

"Maybe it was a wrong number, baby. I don't know any Jennifer Nelson."

"Okay," Regina answered.

Only a few weeks ago, she would've gone fired bombs at Martin for even the possibility of indiscretion, but today, she wanted only for them to continue in the loving direction they were going relationship wise. She convinced herself that it probably was a wrong number.

Martin nearly vomited when he went into the bathroom. How could Jennifer have called him? He'd never given her his phone number. She'd never given him hers. In fact, he'd seen her gloriously naked dozens of times, but he'd yet to see a cell phone, or even a carrying pouch of any kind. She would reach beneath the waistband of her running shorts to extract the keys to the love shack. That was all he'd ever seen. He had to find out the next day. He and Regina were leaving for Chicago after his "run". He'd insisted upon it since he refused to take a chance running alone in the Windy City. He valued his life.

Martin was perplexed when Jennifer wasn't at the River Promenade. He ran home nearly in a dead sprint. He couldn't go to Chicago now. But he had to figure out how to get out of the trip without arousing Regina's suspicion. He stopped at the front door, and put on his best flu-like symptom face. He entered. She emerged from the kitchen. "You're back early. What's wrong?" she asked.

"I don't know. I started feeling sick at the River Promenade, and I walked back home. I almost called you to have to come get me," Martin answered. He faked a dry heave, and ran to the bathroom. He quickly stuck his finger down his throat before Regina arrived. He hadn't eaten since lunch, so his vomit was almost entirely clear fluid. But it was there. He hugged to toilet as if he were in violent pain.

"What can I do, baby?" Regina asked

"I don't know I don't think I can keep anything down. Just help me to the bed."

Regina helped Martin to the bed. He acted as though he were about to die. He had no idea.

"Let me call Chicago and tell them I'm not coming," she said

"No, no. Don't do that. You've been looking forward to this trip all summer, Martin groaned.

"Well, I can't leave you here like this."

"I'll be alright. I think it's just a touch of the flu. It's been going around work."

"Are you sure?"

"Positive. You call me the minute you get there, and if anything comes up with me I'll call you right away."

Regina begrudgingly agreed. She doted over Martin like a mother hen as she prepared to leave for Chicago. It felt as if a week went by, to him, before she was finally ready to go. She finally left. Martin waited an hour. Regina checked on him from West Lafayette. Martin was confident that she was gone. He decided to drive to the love shack, and was about to leave when the doorbell rang. He was sure that it was Regina making sure that he wasn't cheating. If so, he was quite lucky that he hadn't left already. But it wasn't her. It was Jennifer.

"What're you doing here?" he asked as he hustled her inside.

"I came to see you," Jennifer smiled.

"But how do you know where I live, and how did you call my phone?"

"Are you kidding Martin Morris? I've had my eye on you from the first day I saw you on the River Promenade. I had to know everything about you. I'm very resourceful, you know."

"Yeah, and so is Regina."

"She's halfway to Chicago by now."

"I was supposed to go with her."

"I know, Martin. But you stayed because you wanted to see me."

Martin had many more question, but for now, he had to taste her. He picked her up, carried her to his and Regina's bed, and tore her clothes off.

Regina called again when she hit Gary, Indiana, just a half hour outside of Chicago. Martin answered the phone breathlessly.

"Are you okay?" Regina asked

"Yes. I just got finished puking again, but I'm starting to feel better," he answered. Jennifer stared at him lovingly, stroking his once again hardening penis.

156

"Listen. I'm getting a little sleepy now. I think I'll rest, and I'll call you when I wake up," Martin said.

"Okay. I'll call you in the morning if I don't hear from you tonight," she responded. They hung up. Regina, however, had a feeling that she just couldn't shake.

Martin and Jennifer made love three more times over the next two hours. They were both completely spent, feeling as if they were lying on a cloud. "I'd better go," Jennifer said. "I wouldn't want to fall asleep, wake up in the morning, and have your neighbors see me leaving the house." She got up.

"Wait," Martin said. "I want to be with you, Jennifer."

"You were just with me, silly."

"No. I mean I want to be with you forever."

Jennifer sighed. "I love that idea, Martin, but I don't want to hurt Regina."

"You wouldn't be hurting her, I would. Listen. I love Regina, but you hold my heart in your hands."

Jennifer smiled, and Martin's heart was in her hand. They kissed passionately.

Outside, Regina's car pulled in front of the house with the headlights extinguished. The house was dark. She crept up to the front door. She knew that Martin would be angry that she turned around and drove all the way back to Indy, but she would assure him as best she could that it was out of concern for him – assuming he was there, and not out with some chick. She slowly turned the lock, and tipped into the house. She was slapped in the face by what she heard – the moans of a man and a woman in the throes of passionate lovemaking. Her head began to throb like a piston in the engine of a tractor trailer. She could hear the bed squeaking. The same squeaking it had made only the night before, except, at that time, she was in it with the man she loved. She heard Martin call out the bitch's name. Jennifer. Jennifer. Regina became so furious that her vision went blurry. She snuck into the kitchen and removed a butcher's knife from the block. She tipped to the bedroom door. She heard Martin say that he loved Jennifer. Her vision went white as she crashed through the bedroom door.

Regina waited in the holding room before going to arraignment for murder. Her public defender wanted to plead temporary insanity by way of heat of passion, but there was a huge problem.

"Listen, Regina. The police have looked everywhere for Jennifer Nelson. They checked every Jennifer Nelson within a fifty mile radius."

"I know what I heard, man. She was in that room fucking my man."

"Well, all of the Jennifer Nelson's in the search have been cleared by way of age, or airtight alibi, except for one." The lawyer removed a photo from a folder, and showed it to Regina. "Have you seen this woman before?" he asked.

"I told you I never saw the woman. I just heard her. If you bring her down here, I know I'll know her voice. Please bring her down here?"

"That's the problem, Regina. This Jennifer Nelson has been dead for weeks. Her boyfriend apparently drove them off of a bridge and into White River near Broad Ripple."

"Then you need to find the right one. You hear me! Do you hear me!?" Regina broke down into sobs.

The River Promenade was as beautiful as ever. Lovers held hands, and fitness buffs jogged. And at the spot between the two monuments carved into the limestone, if the light was just so, and you looked from the proper angle, and you believed in such things. You could see Jennifer Nelson jogging along, with Martin Morris right by her side.

FOR THE LOVE OF MEENA

A Short Story

By

E. Marvin Neville

The afternoon in Indy brought about the feelings invoked by the onset of spring in the Midwest, even though it was Sunday, October 26, 2008 – the middle of fall. The temperature was fifty-eight degrees, and the strong winds blew dead leaves around so that their fragments looked like brown snow in a dead leaf blizzard. What was even more beautiful to Life Malone was the fact that the winds of true change seemed to be blowing on America, and the world. Though any reasonable voter would have still been fearful, it appeared that – on November 5, 2008 – Barack Obama would be elected the first Black President of the United States, and leader of the free world. Life had tendered his vote early the evening before. He was a part of history.

Life was involved in his normal activities, but his connection to those activities had changed. He watched over his enterprises as much as ever, but he'd ceased to feel as serious about them. They were important, but not as important as before.

Life heard a commotion from the kitchen of his Canal-side restaurant. That wasn't unusual. There seemed always to be spirited disagreements among all of his employees, but even more so from the restaurant where everyone was challenged to make it even better than the best in the city that it already was. He walked into the kitchen. "What's going on that's keeping people from being served food?" he asked.

"Brunch rush is over, Life. We're prepping for dinner hour," Cleveland the chef said.

"Okay, but I'm not seeing prepping. I'm seeing jaw jacking around the door to the dining room."

Benny, the bus boy grinned devilishly at Life. "No, boss, there's a smokin' hot shorty sittin' by herself at a table in the dining room," he said.

Kyle, a waiter, then smiled slyly, and perhaps, overconfidently at Life. "We're trying to decide which one of us has the best chance to get with her," he said.

"I'm gonna have to separate you horny bastards," Life grinned. "Cleveland, your wife Amanda and your three girls, and I'm sure your other children that nobody's sure about, would kill you if you cheat on Amanda because, well, you're doing quite well while she's telling your ass what to do. Benny, the only thing you should be worried about is clearing your parole. So you stick to those crack head hookers we had to call the police to keep from coming up here looking for you. And Kyle, you've got fifteen hours a week at IUPUI. And even though nobody here has a clue what you're majoring in, you're a college student. You can barely afford to buy a postage stamp. You're still having trouble picking up high school girls even when you carry around your IUPUI book bag. So my thinking is that not a single one of you motherfuckers has a chance to even find out the color of her fingernail polish, and each of you has a chance to serve her more than once," Life built to complete laughter.

"That's cold, boss," Cleveland said. "But we still love you. Hey, come take a look at her. I'm willing to bet that even though you're a millionaire, not even you could knock this one out."

"I'd take that bet," Benny laughed. "But you'd have to give me a six month time frame."

"Yeah, not even Laura Bush could resist Life for six months," Kyle giggled.

"Okay, that would be funny, except Laura Bush looks like she could take the pounding she's never had," Life laughed. "I'd have to go for her."

"I'd say bullshit to that, except she's got so much more money than you do that you're probably right," Cleveland smiled. "But you need to check out this chick, boss."

Life walked over to the door between the kitchen and the dining room. He'd barely gotten a glance through the tiny window when he realized that he didn't need any of his group of friends to point the woman they were all salivating over. His knees buckled.

"What's wrong, Life?" Kyle asked. "You know this chick?"

"She's fine, but she ain't enough to make me damn near faint," Benny said.

"Shut up, Benny," Life barked. The entire kitchen quieted as if President George H. W. Bush had just admitted that all of his children had been conceived while he was smoking three eight balls of crack per day. Race was a strange thing. It was a scientifically proven fact that each race had formidable difficulty easily identifying from races different from their own. Life had an even larger problem. He was in still in love with a dead woman from a race that he still had difficulty distinguishing. But the affliction lasted for only a second.

Jassi Gupta, the sister of his late love, Meena Mehta, and the one who'd informed him of the tragic circumstances of her murder by way of her own parents was seated at the table. She was devastatingly beautiful. All four of them watched her as she sipped from a coffee cup – her full lips flaming with red lipstick – as she casually read from a book.

"I'm going out, guys," Life said like a drill sergeant. "Benny, you keep these clowns in the kitchen and you'll walk out of hear with a c-note in your pocket."

"I've got a butcher knife right now, boss."

"Who is she, Life?" Cleveland asked.

"She's the friend of a former friend," Life answered as he strode gallantly through the door. Jassi saw him immediately. Her eyes widened and they looked like dollops of honey dropped into orbs of living white chocolate. She was stunning. She was so obviously Meena's sister that he found himself holding back tears.

"Are you alright, Mr. Malone?" Jassi asked.

"I think I'm well enough to remind you to please not call me Mr. Malone. As far as I'm concerned, we're family, except I'm not Muslim."

"And what are you, Life?"

"The man who's still in love with your sister."

Jassi looked at the floor, holding back her own tears. "She's sorely missed amongst the rest of the family that does not know you," she said sadly.

"What're you doing here, Jassi?"

"This is a restaurant, isn't it?"

"You're right. I'm sorry. Was everything to your satisfaction?"

Jassi smiled. "Are you kidding? The cup of coffee was superb, the service made me feel as if I don't belong here, and the ambiance is special. You must be bathing in one-hundred dollar bills."

That was exactly the type of thing Meena would've said "I don't know about all that, but it definitely sounds good. How are things at home, Jassi?

"They're alright. But they could be a great deal better."

"What do you mean?"

"Well, Mr. Malone – I mean, Life – like Meena, I was raised to be a Muslim wife. Unlike Meena, I'm very good at it. But running the compound is quite a bit harder than I expected. I'm getting some resistance from the males in your secret family. Others are struggling to cope with the changes I'm trying to make."

"That's understandable, Jassi. But I think things will work out in time."

Maybe they will, maybe they won't' Life. But I know how I want things to work out. I want to live like the Muslim families that maintain their faith, but also enjoy the trappings of Western life."

"That's a tough plan. Do you have one?"

"Yes," Jassi smiled. "I choose life."

"What the hell does that mean?"

"You, Life Malone, I choose you."

"Now I understand even less, Jassi."

"Meena loved you so much, Life, and she had very little experience with love. But she didn't love you because you are rich, or because you treated her like a queen. She loved you because you know how to grow things. You cultivated her love for you. You were cultivating the relationship before my parents had her murdered, and you've obviously grown a highly successful business enterprise. I need for you to help me grow my little Muslim family organization. I need for you to teach me to do the same. You know we have money. We can pay you. I don't want to keep having teenagers and young adults working to pay money into our system unless it works like your system.

I want them to go to college, all of them, boys and girls, and I want them to flourish. I want them to learn to grow Western/Muslim/Indian family organizations of their own."

Life wanted to say no. He couldn't. She felt so much like Meena emotionally. And could nearly have been identical twins – at least in his mind's eye. "Nobody can know about this, Jassi."

"I understand. I'm sure you know what I'm up against. India went into action merely hours after my parents and husband was killed. They know that the males here are not ready to lead. They're too young and probably too American, even though some of them try. It'll take time to get them under control, but I have full control of the bank accounts."

"That's good, Jassi. But I feel a but coming."

"As I told you, India is ready to send someone, any male, to marry me, and take over the compound. Needless to say, the man doesn't have to be related to any of us here."

"They can't force you to marry him," Life said.

"You know what they did to Meena. It doesn't matter who owns everything as long as it's a man."

Life understood clearly. He decided to take Jassi Gupta on a journey. He poured over the Mehta/Gupta family books with the electron microscope of his mind. They were good, very good. The vast majority of the income from the two streams he'd discovered when he was with Meena – the farm, and the paychecks of the working. The American economy was tanking, but Life knew that to losses in one financial sector meant huge gains in another in the future. He mostly took the advice of Barack Obama, and sunk disposable cash in America's green future – his own and Jassi's. In the short term, he set up the family finances so that those who tendered their paychecks into the coffers, not only received allowances, but actually owned parts of the business. Many of those who'd objected to Jassi running the business turned in her favor very quickly when they were able to buy their I-pods. But Life took Jassi even farther.

Life took Jassi with him as he solicited votes for Barack Obama from people who'd never voted before – namely those in the underworld where he'd created the origins of his fortune. He introduced her to the world that he'd introduced her younger sister to. He showed her the world where gunfire was accepted as a large part of life, where drug dealers reined stupidly, and where women who didn't want to work for a living had babies by those dealers to get two-streamed income from those dealers and the taxpayers. Jassi never flinched. She greeted baby's mommas and baby's daddies as if they were her own family and she never once did she condescend to them, or ridicule them to Life – at any time, even when he prodded her to do so. In fact, when Life talked badly about them, she defended them. It melted his heart. "I'm really proud of you," he told her after they left a house on Thirty-Second and Ruckle after he'd admonished a local drug dealer for not even having proper identification to vote.

"Why are you proud of me?"

"Well, I've force fed you business regarding the compound, and you've learned fast, Jassi."

"I've listened for many years, Life, and I must say that you have a much better handle on things than any of my relatives. You're a capitalist," she smiled.

"I took you on a fear tour of the toughest spots in Indy, and you never even flinched."

"I was terrified. I almost pissed my pants over on Thirty-Fourth and Keystone. But I was with you. I knew that you would never let anything bad happen to me."

"You left the compound to me if you die, Jassi. I was sure you'd fight me over that."

"Why? There's nobody better suited to make sure that things run right if I'm not here."

"How do you know I won't throw your family on the street and use the compound for my own personal gain?"

"Because then you'd have to hire outsiders to run it, and none of them would want to give part of their earnings to help the compound survive."

Life smiled. "Very good, grasshopper," he said. He stopped at the light at Twenty-First and Capital Avenue, near Methodist Hospital. He looked over at her and smiled. He truly was proud of her. She returned his gaze. Her eyes were bright with self-pride. She was as strong as Meena, and she had the knowledge to achieve her conviction.

"I see very clearly why my sister fell so hard in love with you, Life Malone," she said.

"And why do you think that is?" he asked.

"Make love to me tonight, and I'll tell you, sir."

Had he not been able to still breathe, Life would've thought that his throat had closed. He couldn't remember the last time he'd been so thoroughly speechless. Even in his mind, he stumbled over his words. Jassi could see his awkwardness like a trout could see a worm wiggling on a fish hook. She herself squirmed in her seat. "I'm sorry, Life. I was way out of line," she said.

Life pulled over to the curb and screeched to a halt.

"I know I'm not Meena," Jassi said. "I have two children and I'm trying to do something stupid."

"If you say you're doing something stupid one more time, I'll make you walk home."

"What do you mean?"

"What you're doing for your family is right and just. And, no, you're not Meena. You're Jassi Gupta, and you have power in your own right."

"So why did you just pull off the road and scare me to death?"

"Because Meena would never have apologized about telling me her true feelings"

"She never apologized to you about anything?"

"Sure she did," Life answered calmly. "But even when she thought she was apologizing about her feelings, she wasn't. And she knew it."

"On my death bed, I'll never know what you just said. But I have to ask you, how did she know that?"

"How the hell would I know? I'm just a stupid man who's falling in love for the second time in his life."

Jassi's eyes exploded with happiness. She pounced on Life like a rich cougar at a Chippendale's club. Life simply opened his mouth and let her in. She kissed him so hard that he thought she might burst both of his lips. He was confused. Was he cheating on Meena? Was he with her in a sense? Had Meena merely opened him up to lose control of his emotions? Was Jassi taking advantage of his vulnerability? What did it matter? His dick was harder than trigonometry. It hurt. Jassi broke away from his face. "I'll make love to you right here," she said breathlessly.

"We're on the side of a well-traveled thoroughfare."

"You're a resourceful man, Life. Find someplace."

"It's not just that, Jassi. I mean, this was the last thing I expected to happen. I'm not prepared."

"From what I can feel, you're very prepared," she smiled as she stroked his housed penis.

"I don't have a condom."

Jassi reached into her purse and withdrew four condoms.

"Okay, but I have to check them," Life offered.

"Check them for what?"

"Needle prick holes? It's kind of a habit of mine when the woman brings the condoms."

"What's the matter, Life? You don't want to fuck me?"

"Just the fact that you just said the word fuck makes it impossible for me not to."

Life took Jassi to his house, something that he almost never did. But she was Meena's sister, after all, and he was helping her to better her life and the lives of those around her. On the other hand, he did have his own condoms. Still, the lovemaking was a fumbling affair. It was strange. He'd made love to Meena only once, but the experience was so spectacular that he might well have died for her if it meant that she could live. They'd kissed, groped, and dry fucked a lot before they'd finally made love. But Meena had been so open, so accepting. It was as if she'd been a fierce lover all of her life. With Jassi, on the other hand, her lovemaking seemed more functional. She almost sucked his esophagus into her mouth and masturbated him into ejaculation inside of his pants in the car, but when they finally got naked she was, well, functional. She just let him fuck her. Life wasn't expecting sexual gymnastics, but he was expecting more than what sex was truly intended for – propagating humankind. It was clear that Jassi was a dutiful wife. It was also clear that she wanted more.

On January 20, 2009, two firsts occurred for certain. Barack Obama was sworn in as the first African-American President in American history, and Jassi Gupta had a man's mouth sex her vagina. Before then, only her late husband had even put his mouth on her, and that was to slobber inside of her mouth while he pumped away at her for always less than a minute. Life Malone licked her as if he were creating a work of art on a canvass with his tongue. Jassi gave him a nosebleed when she thrust her hips too hard upon his face during her orgasm. She was becoming addicted to orgasms. She'd never had one before Life Malone. The next night, she asked if she could oral sex him. She'd never done it before, and she wanted to know how it felt. Life explained to her immediately that he wouldn't allow her to suck his dick until she truly felt like it was a labor to genuinely please him. "That's how you get the pleasure," he told her. "You get it by knowing that you're pleasuring your partner."

"Is that why you're so good at sex, Life, because you care only about pleasuring your partner?"

"Well, I wouldn't go so far as to say only, but basically yes. But the key is that you must strike a balance. You want pleasure, and if you put too much pressure on yourself to please your partner, you'll ultimate fail at both."

"So what you're saying is that both partners must make the effort to please their respective partner."

Life smiled. "That's a little clinical, but yes. Let me put it like this. Women require a lot of kissing, and licking, and rubbing, and heavy breathing, and if you tell them you love them, the process is accelerated. That prepares them to be not only penetrated, but to actually have a chance to have an orgasm. Men don't really care about orgasms. They just want to stick their dicks inside of somebody and come. Women have to get wet, and men have to maintain an erection. That's the hard part for a man, no pun intended. Women just have to be lubricated to perform a sex act with reasonable comfort, a man's penis actually has to fill with blood to achieve and maintain an erection."

My husband preferred coconut oil," Jassi giggled.

"Exactly," Life exclaimed. "So, for me, it's always been best to get pleasure from a woman doing the things that most pleasure a woman. May I speak frankly with you?" he asked.

"Of course you may, Life."

"I made love to your sister only once. Before that, it was a whole lot of kissing. But I was good with that because it gave her pleasure."

"You took her virginity?"

"She gave it to me."

Jassi looked away from Life, and then peered deeply into his eyes. "Am I as good a lover as she was, Mr. Malone?" she asked.

"That question is full of dynamite, Mrs.Gupta."

"Do you love me like you loved her?"

"Since it's obvious that I'm not going to be able to escape these explosive questions, let me say this. I loved your sister. I love you. The two of you were different, as was and is my love for you both. But the intensity of my feelings for both of you is equal."

Jassi smiled. "That was really, really good Life Malone. You should've been a love lawyer."

"Your questions only solidify the notion that you feel as strongly about me as I feel about you."

"May I suck your dick now, sir?"

"Just the fact that you said 'suck my dick' makes it so that I can't refuse you."

"Will you tell me if I'm not performing well?"

"I don't see how that could possibly happen."

Life was right. Jassi dove into the effort with confidence, vigor, and the ability to adjust to his non-verbal cues. He didn't like a lot of hand. She figured that out almost immediately, and then she fell into pleasing herself by pleasing him. She looked up at him at one point.

He saw Jassi, but he also saw Meena. She seemed to know that, and she began to pump her head on his shaft like a thirty-year porn star.

By the first day of spring, 2009, Life found himself to be quite happy. He was in love with a fabulous woman, his businesses were doing well even though his investments weren't, but he'd positioned himself to reap the benefits of the financial upturns that he was certain would come about by way of the efforts of Barack Obama. His special phone rang. It was special because it was a pre-paid cell and only two people had ever had the number, and one of them was dead. He picked up. It was Jassi. She was frantic and wanted to meet with him immediately. It was a beautiful day, so they met at the downtown canal at the fountain between St. Claire Street and Walnut Street.

"What's going on, Jassi?"

"My Uncle Sanjay, a man who I've never laid eyes on, is coming here."

"And that means what?"

"He's going to take over the compound."

"He can't do that, Jassi. We own it now."

"The clerics and the Imams don't care, Life. They'll find a way."

"I wouldn't worry about that, baby."

"They want for me to marry him."

"I can't see how I can help you there, Jassi, except to say that they can't force you to day anything. I mean, what do you want me to do, marry you first?"

"Yes. Yes I do. But there's something I need for you to do first."

"Hold up. I'm still stuck back at the marriage thing."

"I need for you to kill him, Life."

"Okay, you're right. That issue does need to be addressed first."

"I saw you're eyes, Life."

"Excuse me?"

"The eyes of the man who shot my late husband are the same ones that look me in my eyes when I arch my back up a little more in bed and let him fuck me in the ass."

"Okay, I see that your mouth has enlisted in the Navy. But let's say for instance that I am the man who shot your husband, and I'm not saying that I am, what's to stop you from killing the next guy, and the next guy, an anybody after that? Maybe somebody cuts you off in traffic, or you don't like the way some chick looks at you, or you're offended by somebody's hair lip."

"Okay, you're just being stupid now."

"I'm being stupid?"

"I know you can do this, Life. And to answer your question, I'm ready to be with you forever if you're ready to be with me. You and I will rule the roost, and everybody in India will know that they can't fuck with us. You know I'm right, Life. You know I am."

"What makes you think I want to marry you, Jassi?"

"Come on, Life. If nothing else, you'll get to look into a face like Meena's every day for the rest of your life. And I'm good with that if it gives me you."

Life looked to the sky. "God, you fucking sailors," he said.

Jassi smiled. "I'm sorry, baby. It's just that I love to say the work fuck. I think I'll use it more."

They both laughed. The planning started immediately after the laughter, even though neither of them spoke about it the following day, and only at their spot at the fountain at the canal. It was a simple plan, really.

The mysterious Uncle Sanjay arrived at Indianapolis International Airport on a crisp March Friday night. Most of Jassi's family was there. Only a few members of the household stayed behind to prepare for the celebration. Life slipped into the basemen. Jassi made certain that the window was unlocked even though he didn't need for her to do so. He could've easily slipped into the basement without even leaving easily seen evidence that he'd done so. He was shocked that the windows hadn't been better secured since he'd used them before. But that wasn't his problem. He hunkered down and waited in a dark corner prepared with two shelves that a person would have to walk up to almost within inches of him to see him. Where Meena had been very innocent, Jassi was very clever. And she showed her cleverness at the airport.

When Uncle Sanjay disembarked into the terminal, the male family members greeted him first, and it was Jassi's turn. She made sure that when she hugged him that their central areas met. He was a good deal taller than her, but she was still able to make the connection. She was learning such good things by being with Life Malone. She held Uncle Sanjay's hand as they rode in the back seat of one of the dozen cars in the caravan, and shamelessly flirted with him like an oversexed school girl. He was hugely surprised. He'd heard about how the financial dynamics had changed at the compound, and he had every intention of restoring the previous economic arrangement of having the younger members work and fork over their respective proceeds. But he'd expected for Jassi to be resistant by at the least giving him the cold shoulder. Instead, she couldn't seem to be able to wait to give over her beautiful, young body to him. He was going to like it in Indiana.

Jassi almost never left Uncle Sanjay's side during the celebration, and after about an hour, she led him to the basement where she slammed her mouth into his and ground her pelvis into his upper thigh in a blatant attempt at dry fucking him. She could barely keep her food down, but the thought of sharing her life with Life Malone kept her stomach acids in their proper place. She then bit his lip, broke away from his face, slapped him hard, and then ran over to where Life was hiding. She smiled devilishly at Uncle Sanjay.

"What are you doing?" he asked angrily as the blood dripped from his lip.

"My late husband used to beat me senseless. The difference between me and most Muslim wives is that I loved it. It made me really hot. Are you hot enough for me, Sanjay?"

Sanjay smiled demonically. He walked over to Jassi and slapped her so hard on her left cheek that saliva exploded out of her mouth. He followed that with a left hook that not only dropped her to the floor, but had broken her jaw. The left hook was unexpected, but it merely bolstered the domestic violence charge she was going to bring against him after he was dead. Self defense was going to change her life. Uncle Sanjay attempted to help her off the floor. That was when Life struck. He tapped Uncle Sanjay on the shoulder as he emerged from the shadows. Life had never seen a man more surprised as he plunged the double edged dagger into a man he'd never met three times in less than two seconds. Life made sure to hit the heart, one lung, and liver. Uncle Sanjay was dead before he hit the floor. Life held the dagger, dripping with blood, out to Jassi with his gloved hand. "Hold this," he said. She took it. He removed a twenty-two caliber automatic pistol from his pocket.

"What's that for?" Jassi asked.

Life slipped the gun into Uncle Sanjay's dead right hand, aimed it at the woman he loved, and fired two shots into her center mass. The look on her face as she collapsed to the floor almost made him cry, but he couldn't leave any DNA behind. He was not her personal killer.

He could not leave her as a loose end, even if they were going to be together. He simply couldn't take the chance.

Life was well off the compound before anybody called the police. He cried two tears as he drove toward his house, one for each of the women he'd ever truly come to love. He didn't care if he ever loved again.

Manufactured By: RR Donnelley
Momence, IL USA
December, 2010